The Interview:

New York

&

Los Angeles

*New York Times, USA Today & Wall Street Journal
bestselling author*

Sandi Lynn

Sandi Lynn

The Interview: New York & Los Angeles

Copyright © 2018 Sandi Lynn Romance, LLC

All rights reserved. No part of this publication may be reproduced, distributed, or transmitted in any form or by any means, including photocopying, recording, or other electronic or mechanical methods without the prior written permission of the publisher.

This is a work of fiction. Names, characters, places and incidents are the products of the authors imagination or are used fictitiously. Any resemblance to actual events, locales, or persons, living or dead, is entirely coincidental.

Cover Photos & Design by Sara Eirew Photography

Cover Models: Lucas Bloms & Gus Smyrnios

Editing by BZ Hercules

The Interview: New York & Los Angeles

Table of Contents

Mission Statement 5
Books by Sandi Lynn 6
Prologue 8
Chapter One 13
Chapter Two 17
Chapter Three 25
Chapter Four 30
Chapter Five 37
Chapter Six 42
Chapter Seven 48
Chapter Eight 54
Chapter Nine 62
Chapter Ten 70
Chapter Eleven 78
Chapter Twelve 84
Chapter Thirteen 90
Chapter Fourteen 92
Chapter Fifteen 97
Chapter Sixteen 103
Chapter Seventeen 109
Chapter Eighteen 118
Chapter Nineteen 123
Chapter Twenty 131
Chapter Twenty-One 136

Chapter Twenty-Two	142
Chapter Twenty-Three	149
Chapter Twenty-Four	154
Chapter Twenty-Five	160
Chapter Twenty-Six	168
Chapter Twenty-Seven	173
Chapter Twenty-Eight	180
Chapter Twenty-Nine	186
Chapter Thirty	194
Chapter Thirty-One	200
Chapter Thirty-Two	205
Chapter Thirty-Three	211
Chapter Thirty-Four	218
Chapter Thirty-Five	225
Chapter Thirty-Six	235
Chapter Thirty-Seven	242
Chapter Thirty-Eight	252
About the Author	261

The Interview: New York & Los Angeles

Mission Statement

Sandi Lynn Romance

Providing readers with romance novels that will whisk them away

to another world and from the daily grind of life – one book at a time.

Books by Sandi Lynn

If you haven't already done so, please check out my other books. Escape from reality and into the world of romance. I'll take you on a journey of love, pain, heartache and happily ever afters.

Millionaires:

The Forever Series (Forever Black, Forever You, Forever Us, Being Julia, Collin, A Forever Christmas, A Forever Family)

Love, Lust & A Millionaire (Wyatt Brothers, Book 1)

Love, Lust & Liam (Wyatt Brothers, Book 2)

Lie Next To Me (A Millionaire's Love, Book 1)

When I Lie with You (A Millionaire's Love, Book 2)

Then You Happened (Happened Series, Book 1)

Then We Happened (Happened Series, Book 2)

His Proposed Deal

A Love Called Simon

The Seduction of Alex Parker

Something About Lorelei

One Night In London

The Exception

Corporate A$$

The Interview: New York & Los Angeles

A Beautiful Sight

The Negotiation

Defense

Playing The Millionaire

#Delete

Carter Grayson (Redemption Series, Book One)

Behind His Lies

Chase Calloway (Redemption Series, Book Two)

Second Chance Love:

Remembering You

She Writes Love

Love In Between (Love Series, Book 1)

The Upside of Love (Love Series, Book 2)

Sports:

Lightning

Prologue

Anti-relationship. That was me. The thought of giving my love and heart to someone for the rest of my life scared me. It wasn't logical. Nothing ever lasts, and in the end, you've given up the person you were to change yourself to who you thought you should be, only to get your heart shattered. You're probably sitting there thinking, "What the hell happened to her to make her feel that way?" So, let me enlighten you.

My parents had been married for thirty years. My father, Jefferson Holloway, was the CEO and owner of Holloway Capital, one of the largest investment firms in Boston. My mother, Adalynn Holloway, was a successful charity event organizer who loved the pretty things in life, including the pool boy who took care of the pool at our six-thousand-square-foot estate; a home in which I grew up and couldn't wait to get the hell out of.

My family was the most dysfunctional family in the world. Well, maybe not in the world, but at least in Boston. Not only was my mother banging the pool boy and her tennis coach, my father was banging anyone who had a vagina. Mid-life crises set in, and as much as they wanted my siblings and me to believe they were happy, they weren't fooling us, or at least me. Divorce wasn't an option. There was too much money and properties involved. Plus, how would it look in their social circle if the Holloway's divorced? Outside the home, they were the perfect couple to everyone. People envied them. My parents could have won Academy Awards for their stellar performances. Did I mention that my mother liked to drink?

The Interview: New York & Los Angeles

Tequila was her beverage of choice these days. The simplicity of wine just wasn't cutting it for her.

My brother, Alfie, age twenty-five, who was every girl's orgasm with his clean-cut sandy blond hair, green eyes, light stubble around his jawline, and his six-foot-one, muscular stature, lived up to my father's expectations and followed in his footsteps, working side by side with him at Holloway Capital. Me? I worked as a journalist for the *Seattle Times* writing for an advice column called "Everything Laurel," which ranged from anything relationships to etiquette and self-help.

George, my best friend, thought I'd be the perfect fit, so he talked to his boss, Eric. Plus, he owed me since I saved his ass from a deranged sorority girl who was out to kill him after he broke up with her back in college. I wasn't kidding about the killing part. She was a broken-hearted, obsessed girl who thought she was madly in love with him. One day, she went and got herself a 9mm and pointed it directly at him. If I hadn't shown up to his apartment that night he was being held at gunpoint, he'd be dead because she was crazy enough to pull the trigger. Fortunately, I was studying psychology as my minor and was able to talk her out of it and get her the help she needed. I always wondered what happened to her once she left Boston University. So yeah, George owed me big time for saving his life and things couldn't have worked out more perfect taking a job over three thousand miles away from my dysfunctional family.

Not only did I have a brother, but I also had a twenty-year-old sister named Bella, who looked exactly like Alfie with her blonde hair and green eyes. I was the odd girl out with brown hair and blue eyes. Where did I get that from, you ask? My birth parents. See, Jefferson and Adalynn were my adoptive parents. They adopted me when I was three weeks old because my mother was told she could never have children after three years of IVF treatments. Then two years later, she became pregnant with Alfie. It was a miracle, and even more a miracle, five years after Alfie, when Bella joined our family. Since my mother wasn't taking any more chances on these "surprise" pregnancies, my father decided to get a vasectomy. He insisted after my mother had told him she was getting her tubes tied. Clever on his part, because then he wouldn't have to worry about getting any of the women he had affairs with pregnant.

Bella was a student at Juilliard. She had been accepted right after she graduated high school at the age of seventeen. Her dream after Juilliard was to join one of the top dance companies in the world. We weren't as close as two sisters should be, probably because of our seven-year age difference or the fact that when she started dancing at the age of three, life revolved around her.

Now that you have the background story on my family, back to my anti-relationship issue. First, there are some things you need to know about me. My name is Laurel Holloway, I'm twenty-seven years old, I've been someone's girlfriend once in my life and I love sex. Sex with guys where there's no chance of getting emotionally attached, usually one-night stands. I have plenty of friends and I love to go out and have a good time. It's hard to imagine that one experience in your life could alter the way you see things forever. After much debate with myself at the age of eighteen about getting into a relationship, I finally gave in and became the girlfriend of David Hampton, an aspiring musician who I met my freshman year at Boston University. He swept me off my feet and made me feel like I was the only woman in the world. I fell for him hard and fast. We had dated for almost a year, spending every moment we could together. I shared a room with my childhood best friend, Marissa. We were inseparable since the age of seven and knew each other's deepest secrets. The one secret I didn't know about her was that she was sleeping with my boyfriend and had been for over two months of our relationship. It was just as much David's fault as it was hers. Would you like to hear the gory details of how I found out? I thought you would.

I had gone home for the weekend because it was Bella's birthday and my mother threw her a big birthday bash. I had

The Interview: New York & Los Angeles

asked David to come with me and he said with finals coming up, he needed to stay back and study. So, I left on Friday after my classes and decided to go back early Sunday to surprise him. Now, in the meantime, he had been texting me all weekend saying how much he loved me and missed me. He really knew how to set my heart on fire and I truly believed that we would be together forever. Stupid, I know. I decided to stop at my dorm room and change before going over to his frat house and surprising him. When I opened the door, the only thing I saw was him fucking Marissa while she was bent over the bed and him saying over and over again, "I love you." Shock swept over me as my heart began to pound so hard, I thought my chest was going to explode. I stood there and stared at them while my perfectly happy heart broke in half. The pain that coursed through me was the worst pain I had ever felt in my life. Tears filled my eyes as I took in a deep breath, turned, and walked away. David ran after me wearing only his jeans, and when I exited the building doors, he grabbed my arm and told me he was sorry and that it would never happen again. I never did forgive him or Marissa.

After many hours of walking around, crying, and staring out the window of a café while sipping on a latte I wished so badly was filled with alcohol, I went back to my room, packed up all my things, and told Marissa she could have him. That was the day I met George. He saw me loading up my car and walked over and helped me. He introduced himself, and we spent the rest of the night talking, or should I say, me crying on his shoulder. He had an apartment not too far from my dorm and he told me that I could stay there as long I needed to. I couldn't go home, because if I did, I'd have to explain to my parents what happened, and I didn't want to do that, plus I couldn't miss my classes. That was the day my heart was broken for the very first time, and I lost the love of my life and my best friend. But some good came from it. George and I had become best friends and best friends only. Not best friends with benefits. There were never any romantic feelings between the two of us, just respect and a good solid friendship. That was also the day I closed off my heart again, but this time forever.

George Locke was one year older than I was and graduated before me. As soon as he left Boston University, he went back home to Seattle where a journalist position was waiting for him. It also helped that his dad's best friend owned the *Seattle Times*. We kept in touch almost every day and I flew out there a few times to visit him. After I graduated, I took a part-time job at a local newspaper in Boston, but that only lasted six months before they shut down. I ended up doing some freelance work for small magazines for a few months before George called me and offered me a job in Seattle. I was on that like a bee on honey. I needed to get out of Boston and away from the constant badgering of my mother asking me what I was going to do with my life and why I didn't have a boyfriend, while she sat there and kicked back her tequila at twelve in the afternoon.

I ended up staying with George and Kairi, his then girlfriend, for a couple of weeks until I found an apartment. I got settled, started my new job, and have been as happy as a clam for the past four years, living life on my own and exactly how I wanted.

The Interview: New York & Los Angeles

Chapter One

Los Angeles Bound

"Laurel, I need to see you in my office," my boss Eric spoke.

Getting up from my chair, I walked in and took a seat across from his desk.

"What's up, Eric?" I asked.

"Congratulations. You're getting a promotion."

"Wow. Really?" A wide grin graced my face.

"Yes. You know how we've started the ball on our new magazine, *Fusion Daily*?"

"Yeah."

"We want you to write articles for it and we've decided that we're going to switch Everything Laurel to the magazine from the paper. We believe that it will help to gain traffic and sales."

"Okay. Do you have any specific topics for the articles?"

"Actually, I do. We thought it would be a good idea to interview some well-known bachelors."

"Huh?" I arched my brow.

"Not just any bachelors." He pointed at me. "Bachelors that

are self-made millionaires under the age of thirty-five and very successful in what they do. I want you to find out what makes them tick and why they haven't settled down. I think it would make for an interesting read, especially for the ladies."

"And what makes you think they'd tell me?"

"Come on, Laurel, you're a journalist. It's your job to get that information out of them. Plus, you're a beautiful woman. Throw on a sexy dress and some high heels, and draw them in."

I rolled my eyes. "Do you have certain bachelors in mind?"

He pushed a piece of paper to the edge of his desk.

"We took a poll."

Taking hold of it, I studied each name and occupation. The list consisted of two men: Craig Pines, head chef and owner of Rosie's in Los Angeles, and Wyatt Coleman, owner and CEO of Coleman Enterprises in New York.

"They're both successful, young, and single." Eric smiled.

"And they're very rich men." I smirked.

"Exactly! And that's why women want to know why they're still single. Start with Craig Pines in California and then head to New York. You have one week. Get to know them, interview them, find out their secrets, and write your stories."

"Okay, then." I sat there nodding my head. "Do you think one week will be enough time for both?"

"Get in and get out."

"When do you want me to leave?"

"As soon as possible. Take a couple days to get packed and be on your way. In the meantime, don't neglect Everything Laurel."

The Interview: New York & Los Angeles

"What about flight arrangements and hotels?" I asked.

"You can do all that yourself. Use the company account. I'll have Shari give you the company American Express card to use for food and incidental expenses. Just don't go overboard."

I arched my brow. "You do realize how expensive California and New York are, right?"

He sighed. "Yes, I know. Just spend wisely. Maybe you only need two meals a day. On second thought, get the billionaires to buy you dinner. They can afford it."

Rolling my eyes, I got up from my seat. "I'll let you know when I'm leaving," I spoke as I walked out the door.

Looking at my watch, I saw it was lunchtime and I decided to leave the office and go home to start making arrangements for my trips. Walking to my car, I pulled my phone from my pocket and dialed George, who was in Florida working on a story.

"Hello, sunshine."

"Guess who's going out of town?" I smiled as I walked to my car.

"Would that be you?"

"Yes. Eric is sending me to California and New York."

"Lucky bitch! Why?"

"To interview two young, single, and successful millionaires." I climbed into my car and shut the door.

"Wow. Is that for the magazine?" he asked.

"Yes."

"When are you leaving?"

"In a couple days. When are you getting back?"

"My flight gets in Thursday afternoon at two o'clock."

"Maybe I can coordinate with your schedule and we can meet up at the airport before I board. Maybe have lunch or something."

"That would be great. Hey, I have to go. I'm being summoned."

"Have fun and stay safe. I'll talk to you soon."

When I arrived home, I poured myself a glass of wine, opened my laptop, and looked up flights to Los Angeles. Picking up the phone, I dialed Rosie's.

"Good afternoon. Thank you for calling Rosie's. How can I help you?"

"Hello, I would like to speak with Craig Pines, please."

"May I ask who's calling?"

"This is Laurel Holloway with the *Seattle Times*. I would like to set up an interview with Mr. Pines."

"Hold one moment, please."

As I listened to the boring elevator music on the other end, I lightly tapped my fingernails against my desk.

"I'm sorry, but Mr. Pines is not interested in doing an interview. Thank you for calling." *Click.*

Seriously? I set my phone down and booked my flight to Los Angeles anyway. I tried to do it the professional way, but since he declined, I'd have to go another route.

The Interview: New York & Los Angeles

Chapter Two

I arrived in Los Angeles Thursday afternoon at three o'clock. I couldn't get a flight that coincided with George's arrival, so I didn't get to see him before I left. After picking up my luggage from baggage claim, I called an Uber to take me to my hotel: Four Seasons Los Angeles. I knew it was pricey, but Eric did say to make my own arrangements. Plus, it was right across the street from Rosie's.

After settling in and staring out at the magnificent view of L.A. from my hotel window, I dialed the restaurant to make a dinner reservation.

"Good afternoon. Thank you for calling Rosie's. How may I help you?"

"I would like to make a dinner reservation for tonight."

"I'm sorry, but we're all booked up."

"How about for tomorrow night?" I asked with irritation.

"I'm sorry, but reservations are full."

I let out a deep sigh. "Thank you."

I needed to think, and I needed to think fast. I wasn't shy about doing underhanded things. I needed to get into the restaurant and at least meet Mr. Pines first before I sprang on him who I really was and why I was there. He was going to give me an interview, no matter what I had to do to get it.

After finishing my shower, I applied my makeup, threw some soft curls into the ends of my long brown hair, and stepped into a strapless white maxi dress. Grabbing my handbag from the bed, I headed across the street to the restaurant.

When I walked through the large glass doors with "Rosie's" proudly written in gold across them, I was greeted by a younger blonde woman.

"Hello. How may I help you?" She smiled.

"I'm meeting someone here." My eyes scanned the restaurant.

"Okay. The name of the person you're meeting?"

Looking over to my left, I saw a round table with two younger men sitting down. Perfect. They wouldn't mind if I horned in on their dinner.

"Oh. I see them." I smiled as I walked away.

"Miss, wait." The hostess followed behind.

When I approached the table, the two handsome men stopped their conversation and looked up at me.

"I'm so sorry I'm late." I planted a kiss on the cheek of the man with the perfectly styled black hair and then moved on to his friend with the longer brown curly hair.

Both men stared in confusion at me as I took a seat across from them.

"Traffic was horrible." I waved my hand in the air.

"Umm," the man with the black hair spoke.

"Sir, is she with you?" the hostess asked.

He looked at me as the corners of my mouth curved up into a cunning smile.

The Interview: New York & Los Angeles

"Yes. Yes, she is," the brown curly-haired man spoke with a grin. "We just weren't sure if she was going to be able to make it." He winked at me.

The hostess handed me a menu and then scurried off to seat the line of people that had filtered through the door after me.

"Hi." I smiled as I held out my hand. "I'm Laurel Holloway."

The black-haired man gently placed his hand in mine. "I'm Dean Howell. And this is Brett Sommers."

"Nice to meet you both. I'm so sorry for intruding on your dinner, but I needed to get into this restaurant tonight and all reservations were full."

"Do you always just invade other people's tables when you can't get a reservation?" Brett smirked.

"No. This is my first time, and the two of you looked like nice gentlemen who wouldn't mind."

"You're right. We would never turn down the company of a beautiful woman." Dean smiled.

"I'm sure your wives would disagree." I scanned their left fingers and noticed the gold bands they were wearing.

"May I get you something to drink?" The waitress walked over.

"I'll have a neat martini, straight up with two olives."

"Coming right up." She smiled.

"Excellent choice of drink." Dean winked.

"Okay, fellas, let me let you in on a little secret. I'm a journalist with the *Seattle Times* and I'm hoping to secure an interview with the owner of this restaurant."

"Wouldn't a simple phone call have been easier?" Brett

asked.

"I called. He declined. Hence the reason why I'm sitting here with you two gentlemen."

"So, you're using us?" Dean smirked.

"Yes. I guess I am. You didn't honestly think I just sat down here to persuade you to have sex, did you?" I arched my brow.

The waitress returned and set my martini down in front of me.

"Are you ready to order?"

"I'll have the sourdough crusted king salmon and the market mushroom salad." I handed her the menu. "So?" I cocked my head as I looked at Dean and Brett. "You didn't answer my question."

Both men cleared their throats for they weren't quite sure how to answer.

"No, of course not." Brett chuckled. "We're happily married men. We would never."

"I'm sure you wouldn't." I took a sip of my martini. "Go ahead and finish the conversation you were having before I sat down. Don't mind me. I'll just be sitting here minding my own business."

As I looked around the restaurant, I couldn't help but notice how elegantly decorated it was. High back, private leather booths lined the walls with just enough seating for two people, all enclosed by cherry wood dividers to give the utmost privacy. Round tables with crème-colored leather chairs filled the rest of the space and were draped with white linens and burgundy runners. Finally, after about forty-five minutes, my food was served.

"Enjoy." The waitress smiled as she set my plate in front of me.

The Interview: New York & Los Angeles

Brett and Dean finished up their drinks and got up from their seats.

"It was a pleasure to make your acquaintance, Laurel." Brett smiled.

"Indeed, it was," Dean spoke. "Good luck getting that interview."

"Thank you, gentlemen, and I'm sorry for intruding on your dinner."

"No worries. It was fun." Dean smiled as they both walked away.

Taking a bite of my salmon, I savored the mouthwatering taste. It was delicious and the best salmon I had ever had.

"How's your meal?" the waitress asked.

"May I ask who the chef is?"

"That would be Mr. Pines. Is something wrong?"

"Actually, this salmon is very dry and I'm not happy," I lied. "I would like to speak with the chef. Considering this is a five-star restaurant, I would expect the salmon not to be dry."

"I'm very sorry, miss. Let me go talk to the chef and I'll bring you another one."

"I would like to speak with him myself. Could you please tell him that a customer is very dissatisfied with her meal?"

"Of course. I'll be right back." She took away my plate.

Shit. I was hungry and wanted to finish the delicious salmon that was in front of me, but I couldn't.

"Excuse me. Jennifer tells me that something is wrong with the salmon I prepared," a brutally handsome man who stood about six feet two with brown hair, piercing blue eyes, and very muscular arms spoke.

"Yes. It's dry."

"Impossible." He cocked his head with a small smile.

"Not impossible." I held up my finger. "I would like to speak with the owner of this restaurant, please. I'm a customer and the customer is always right." I narrowed my eye at him.

"I am the owner and you're right, the customer is always right. Let me prepare another salmon for you."

"Only if you promise to bring it out yourself." I smirked.

"I'm very busy tonight. Look around. My restaurant is packed full."

"I can see that, but if you want a satisfied customer…"

"I'll see what I can do. By the way, may I ask your name?"

"Laurel." I held out my hand.

"I'm Craig Pines. It's nice to meet you." He placed his hand in mine.

I watched as his fine ass in tight black pants walked away. Damn. Dirty thoughts were scrambling in my head faster than a race car raced around the track. About fifteen minutes later, Craig walked up and set a plate of salmon in front of me.

"I hope this one meets your expectations." He gently smiled.

Picking up my fork, I placed it in the salmon and took a bite.

"It's perfect. Thank you."

"I'm happy you're pleased. Now if you'll excuse me, I have other meals to prepare."

"Hey, Craig," I spoke as he began to walk away. "How about a drink after you close up?"

The Interview: New York & Los Angeles

He turned and looked at me. "I know who you are, Miss Holloway, and I'm not doing an interview." He smirked as he went back into the kitchen.

Shit. I bit down on my bottom lip as I sat there and devised my next plan. I looked at the time on my phone. It was nine o'clock. Two hours and the restaurant would be closing. After finishing my dessert, which was out of this world, I paid my bill and went and sat up at the bar where I would stay until they kicked me out. One way or another, I was going to talk to Craig Pines again.

"Laurel, we're closing up now," the bartender named Barney spoke.

"And?" I raised my brow.

"You have to leave."

"I will as soon as I finish up my drink." I frowned.

"You've been nursing that drink for the last hour. Don't you have anywhere else you need to be? Don't you have any friends?"

"Yes, I have friends. They all happen to be back in Seattle."

"And you're still here." Craig took a seat next to me at the bar.

"Yes, I am." I nodded. "I'm just finishing up this martini and then I'll leave."

"Good. Have a good night." He got up and walked away.

I sighed as I finished off my martini.

"Hey." Barney leaned over the bar. "You didn't hear this from me. Every morning at seven o'clock, Craig goes to Venice Beach to do some surfing."

"He surfs?" My eyes widened.

23

"He does."

"Thanks, Barney."

"Now get out of here so I can go home." He smiled.

The Interview: New York & Los Angeles

Chapter Three

The buzzing sound of the alarm woke me from a deep sleep. Reaching over and grabbing my phone, I shut it off and stretched across the comfy bed. Once I mustered the energy to get up, I threw on a pair of shorts and a tank top and threw my hair into a ponytail. Slipping my feet into my sandals, I headed down to the lobby where an Uber was waiting for me.

"Where to?" the driver asked.

"Venice Beach, please."

As I approached the sand, I took off my shoes and carried them while I walked down to the shoreline. Looking out at the beautiful blue ocean, I saw there were several surfers in the water. How the hell did I know which one was him? I couldn't tell, so I planted myself down in the sand and took in the warm breeze that swept across me and watched as the surfers attempted to ride the waves. Some were really good; others, not so much. As I was taking in the peaceful morning, my phone rang, and George was calling.

"Good morning, George."

"Morning, sunshine. I didn't wake you, did I?"

"Nope. I'm sitting in the sand at Venice Beach right now."

"What? Why?"

"Because Mr. Pines is here surfing. He declined the interview last night, so I had to figure out another way to get his attention."

"So, you're stalking him?"

"Pretty much. I'm getting that interview one way or another."

"That's my girl. Good luck. I have to run. I just wanted to check in. I'm having breakfast with Veronica before I head to the office."

"Tell her I said hi."

"I will. Be safe, Laurel."

"Talk to you soon, George."

Veronica was George's new girlfriend. They had been dating a few months and I really liked her. She was a lot better than the previous girls he had dated. It just so happened that her best friend was a guy, so she understood our relationship. The others didn't. It was their insecurities that drove George away. As I set my phone down, I looked up to see Craig walking towards me with his surfboard under his arm.

"Miss Holloway?"

"Mr. Pines. Fancy seeing you here. Good morning." I smiled.

"What are you doing here?" he asked.

"Enjoying the beach. What are you doing here?"

He looked at his surfboard and then at me.

"Right." I smirked. "You're surfing. Wow. I didn't know you surfed."

"How would you?" He cocked his head.

The Interview: New York & Los Angeles

"I wouldn't."

"So, this is just a coincidence, us running into each other here?"

"What are you insinuating?" I got up.

"I just think it's strange seeing you here this morning," he replied.

"Really? I'm not allowed to sit on this public beach while I'm in California because you're here?" I spoke with an attitude.

"If you only came here to sit on the beach, it's fine, but if you came here to see me, it's not."

Putting up my hand, I began to walk away. "I didn't know this was your beach. I'll find another one to sit on." I angrily walked away but with a smile on my face.

"Are you hungry?" he shouted from a few feet away.

I stopped, turned around, and looked at him. "Why?"

"There's this diner on the boardwalk that serves great breakfast. I'm heading there now if you'd like to join me."

"Are you sure? I'd hate to ruin your day any further."

"Come on, Laurel. You aren't ruining my day and if I didn't want you to join me, I wouldn't have asked."

I silently smiled to myself. I was getting this interview.

"I'd love to join you. Thank you."

Craig and I walked to his car so he could take his wetsuit off and slip on a t-shirt. When he took the wetsuit down, my ovaries may have exploded a little. His body was ripped in all the right places. It took great control and inner strength not to reach out and touch him. We made our way to the diner and sat down in a booth by the window overlooking the beach.

"Tell me about yourself," Craig spoke as he sipped on his coffee.

"Well, I grew up in Boston and I have a brother and a sister." I smiled.

"And?"

"That's pretty much it. You already know I work for the *Seattle Times*."

"Why Seattle?" he asked.

"It was the furthest place away from my family." I held the white coffee cup between my hands.

"Ah." He lightly nodded his head. "I take it you and your family aren't close?"

"Not really. My mother likes to nag, drink, and bang the pool boy, and my father is a workaholic who likes to bang anyone who has a vagina."

"Oh. I don't know what to say to that." He smirked.

"I don't blame you. I wouldn't know what to say either if someone told me that."

The waitress walked over, set our breakfast down in front of us, and refilled our cups.

"How did you end up owning your own restaurant?" I asked nonchalantly.

His eyes narrowed at me as he took a bite of his eggs.

"Are you interviewing me, Miss Holloway?"

"No. I told you about me, so I would like to know a little about you."

He sighed. "As much as I would like to tell you about myself, I'm afraid I can't."

The Interview: New York & Los Angeles

"Why?"

"Because it will end up in an article."

"People want to know about you, Craig. You're a star. You should be proud of what you've accomplished at your age, and most importantly, women want to know why nobody has snatched you up yet."

"That's nobody's business," he snapped.

I sat there and stared at him as he looked away from me. I was good at reading people, and something told me he was hiding something. Maybe he was gay. Yeah, he was gay and didn't want anyone to know. But he didn't have to snap at me the way he did.

"I'm sorry. I didn't mean to—"

"Don't apologize, Laurel. I'm sorry for the tone I used. It's just I keep my personal life very private and that's how I want it to stay."

"Okay, then. How about this. Let's do a day or a week in the life of Craig Pines. I'll be your shadow and you can show me what you do from day to day. Kind of like a behind the scenes at the restaurant. We'll give people a glimpse of your life without the personal stuff. It'll do wonders for the restaurant. Not that you need it. Plus, maybe you'll inspire someone who wants to own their own restaurant."

"No personal stuff?"

"Just business. Deal?" I held out my hand to him.

"Deal." The corners of his mouth curved upwards as he placed his hand in mine.

"To the start of a new friendship." I smiled as I held up my coffee cup.

"Indeed." He grinned.

Chapter Four

"Where are you staying?" Craig asked as we climbed into his car.

"Four Seasons."

"Right across the street from the restaurant?"

"Yep."

"I need to change before heading there, so we'll stop at my place first and then I'll take you back to the hotel."

"Oh. You're inviting me to your home?" I smiled.

"Yes, actually, I am. That is, if you don't mind."

"Not at all. I'd love to see your place."

We had only driven a little over a mile before he pulled into the Del Rey Marina.

"Are we doing some boating first?" I asked.

"No. This is where I live." His lips formed a smile.

"Huh?" I arched my brow at him.

"I live on a boat."

"Get out!" I lightly smacked his arm and he chuckled.

The Interview: New York & Los Angeles

He pulled into a parking spot and then led me to his sixty-five-foot coastal cruiser.

"Welcome to my home, Laurel." He smiled as he held out his hand and helped me aboard.

While he went to his bedroom to change, I looked around and admired the beauty of his place. The dark cherry wood trim was stunning. The kitchen was pretty big with cherry wood cabinets and black granite countertops with a hint of gold swirled throughout. The living area consisted of a beige sectional, rectangular coffee table, two matching chairs, and a seventy-inch TV that hung perfectly on the wall above the fireplace. It was comfortable and inviting, and I could totally see myself living here.

"So, what do you think?" Craig asked as he entered the living area.

"I think it's great. I've never known anyone who lived on a boat full-time."

"Would you like to see the rest of it?"

"I'd love to." I smiled as he led the way. "I bet the women you bring here love it."

"I don't really bring women here."

"Guys?" I bit down on my bottom lip.

"Excuse me?" His eye narrowed at me. "Do you think I'm gay, Laurel?"

"No." I quickly turned away as I looked in the bathroom.

"Yes, you do. Is that what you're trying to get out of me?"

"No, Craig. Not at all. I apologize," I spoke as I glanced at him.

Our eyes locked onto each other's for a moment. His stare

was haunting and sexy. He was sexy. Before I knew it, he approached me and placed both of his hands on each side of my face while his mouth smashed into mine. His lips soft, yet his kiss rough. I kissed him back. I had to. He was too good not to.

He broke our kiss and placed his forehead against mine. "I'm not gay."

"Okay," I gulped.

Well, so much for that. Now I was really curious as to why he wasn't taken. Especially with the way he kissed. *Shit.*

"We better get going. I have to get to the restaurant," he spoke. "I'll drive you to your hotel so you can change clothes."

We climbed into his car and he drove me back to the hotel and waited for me while I changed. I could still feel his lips against mine.

"Don't put on anything nice. You're going to get it dirty."

"What?" I poked my head around the corner of the bathroom door.

"You're going to be helping me prepare food." He smiled.

I let out a laugh. "I don't cook. Trust me, you don't want me helping."

"Then I'll teach you. And how can you not cook? What do you do for meals?"

"I eat out a lot. We had a chef growing up, so I never bothered to learn."

"Ah. That explains it."

After changing into a pair of khaki capris and a different tank top, I walked over to where he was standing.

"Is this okay?" I asked as I did a full turn.

The Interview: New York & Los Angeles

"It's perfect."

We climbed into his car and drove across to the restaurant. As soon as we reached the kitchen, Craig handed me an apron and introduced me to his staff.

"Everyone, this is Laurel Holloway. She's going to be shadowing us for a while for an article she's doing on the restaurant. Laurel, this is Jack, Melanie, Chris, Big Tom, and Selena."

"Nice to meet you all." I waved.

"You can start by mixing up this dough," he spoke as he set a bowl down in front of me. "Go wash your hands first."

"Huh? I thought you were kidding when you said I'd be helping you."

"How can you write a good article if you don't become a team player?" His brow arched.

"Umm. Sure. Okay." I walked over to the sink and washed my hands. "So, what do you want me to do again?" I asked.

"Put your hands in the bowl, mix the dough, and form it into a ball."

Placing my hands in the large stainless-steel bowl, I began to work all the ingredients together the best I could.

"This doesn't seem to be working."

Craig let out a light laugh. "Here," he spoke as he came up from behind me, placed his hands on mine, and we worked the dough together.

A feeling overtook me. I liked his hands on mine and his body so close to me. There was something about what we were doing that felt erotic. Who knew mixing dough could be like that.

"It's all in the rhythm," he spoke as our hands manipulated the dough. "Got it?"

"I think so." I looked back at him and smiled.

He slowly removed his hands from mine and told me to keep the motion going. As my hands were buried in dough, I watched him as he ordered his staff around. Not in a bossy type of way, but in a fun and friendly way. I could tell they were like a family.

"I think you're done," Craig spoke as he examined the bowl of dough.

"Thank God. My hands were cramping up."

"You did good, Laurel," he spoke as he took the dough out of the bowl and set it on some large plastic-looking thing.

"Thank you. These hands can work magic on just about anything." I smirked with an arch in my brow.

"I'm sure they can." He winked.

While I was standing off to the side watching how Craig ran his kitchen, I couldn't stop thinking about his "I'm not gay" kiss. The warmth of his lips made my body tremble in delight.

"Are you writing all this down?" Craig glanced over at me. "Because I don't see you taking notes."

"I don't need to write things down," I lied. "It's all up here." I tapped the side of my forehead.

He gave me smile as he walked out of the kitchen. I quickly ran over to the large man they called Big Tom.

"Hey." I smiled. "Do you know why Craig is still single?" I batted my eyelashes at him.

"I really couldn't tell you. But, if I had to guess, it would be because he spends every waking moment of his life in here."

The Interview: New York & Los Angeles

"Really?" I frowned.

"Yeah. That houseboat he lives on, it isn't home. This is his home."

"Interesting. Thanks." I patted his back.

Craig walked back into the kitchen and narrowed his eye at me.

"And what would the two of you be talking about?" he asked.

"He was showing me how he chops these vegetables so fast. Amazing."

"Was he now? Listen, Laurel, I was thinking about taking tonight off. Why don't you swing by my place around seven and I'll cook us up some dinner?"

"Well, well, Mr. Pines. You're inviting me to your home for dinner? I thought you don't do that sort of thing."

"I usually don't, but since you came to town for me, I figured it would be a nice gesture since you aren't getting any personal information out of me." He smiled. "I would hate to think that your trip was wasted."

"And how is it you can take the night off? I thought you worked 24/7."

"I occasionally take a night off. But only if I have a reason to."

"So, you're saying that I'm your reason." I smirked.

"Yes. I guess I am. Don't read too much into it, though."

"I won't. I'm going to head back to the hotel. I'll see you at seven o'clock," I spoke as I turned around and walked away.

Craig Pines was definitely a charmer. Hot, sexy, and a

charmer all mixed in one delicious package. Now my curiosity was more piqued than ever. Why was this successful, sexy, charming man still single at the age of thirty-four?

The Interview: New York & Los Angeles

Chapter Five

The moment I entered my hotel room, my phone rang with a facetime call from Eric.

"Eric, I was just going to call you."

"How's it going with Craig Pines?" he asked as he leaned back in his oversized brown leather chair.

"He's a tough cookie. I'm going to need a couple of extra days. He's not willing to do a personal interview, so I suggested a day/week in the life. I just got back from being behind the scenes in his kitchen at the restaurant."

I noticed he was bobbing his head back and forth, trying to make out the details of my hotel room.

"What hotel are you staying at?" he asked.

"Why do you want to know?" I narrowed my eye at him.

"That looks like the Four Seasons. I thought I told you not to go overboard."

"His restaurant is right across the street. Think of the money I'm saving on cab fare, Eric. If you want these interviews, we can't look cheap. I have to play the part. After all, these are millionaires I'm dealing with."

"Well, for what that hotel is costing me and now you're saying you need a couple more days, you better get that damn interview." He pointed at me.

"Don't worry. He invited me over to his houseboat for dinner tonight."

"Good girl. Keep me posted."

"I will." I walked into the bathroom. "I have to go, Eric. This luxurious bathtub is calling my name." I grinned as I turned the camera around and then ended the call.

After starting the water and pouring two capfuls of rose-scented bubble bath into the tub, I twisted up my hair, stripped out of my clothes, and climbed in. One of the best ways to try and get some information on Craig Pines was to ask his boat neighbors. They had to know something about him. After my bath, I climbed on the bed with my laptop and looked to see if there were any boats for sale at the marina. I needed to be sneaky. To my surprise, there was. Picking up my phone, I dialed the number that was listed.

"Hello," a firm voice answered.

"Hello, I'm inquiring about the boat you have for sale."

"Ah yes. What would you like to know?"

"I would love to come see it in person. I'm sure the pictures you have online don't do it justice."

"No, they don't. When would you like to come?"

"Now if possible. I'm only in town for one more day."

"I see. Umm. Sure, now will be fine. Let me give you the address."

"Great. I'll see you soon."

After ending the call, I took an Uber to the marina and found that the boat that was for sale was docked three spots down from Craig's. As I was approaching the boat, an older gentleman was

The Interview: New York & Los Angeles

standing on the deck staring at me.

"Are you the one who called about seeing the boat?" he asked.

"I am." I smiled as I stepped onto the deck. "Laurel Holloway."

"Where's your husband?" he asked.

"I don't have a husband." I laughed.

"So, you're the one who wants to buy a boat?"

"Yes. Is there something wrong with that?" I asked in confusion.

"Well, no. I'm just curious as to how you can afford something like this. The price was listed."

I stood there, biting down on my lower lip, trying to control my tongue, which wanted to lash out at this male chauvinist pig.

"I'm sorry, but did you not catch my name?" I cocked my head. "I'm Laurel Holloway of Holloway Capital in Boston."

"Oh gee. I'm sorry, Miss Holloway. I didn't realize. Let's have a look around, shall we?" His tone changed.

I only had to use my family's name and status when I needed to, no matter how much it killed me to do it.

"This is lovely. Why are you selling?" I asked.

"I'm moving to New York for business."

"Nice. New York is a lovely place." I looked around. "One concern I do have is the surrounding people in the area. I like quiet. So, if there are any neighbors of yours that are loud or like to party excessively, I need to know."

"Trust me, Miss Holloway, it's very quiet here. Not a lot of people live on their boats full-time. There's really only one person, at least on this side of the marina, who does and that would be Mr. Pines. Are you looking to live on a boat full-time?"

"I am. I want adventure and I think boat living is one." I smiled. "So, tell me about Mr. Pines. Is he noisy?"

"Nah." He grinned. "Mr. Pines is an excellent guy. Single too. In fact, I think the two of you would get along real well."

"Single, you say?" My brow raised.

"Yeah. He keeps to himself. An occasional hi or wave here and there. That's about it. He's hardly ever home. He owns a restaurant."

"Fascinating. I'm sure with him being a restaurant owner and being single, he must have a slew of women coming and going."

"Not really. He's mostly a loner, to be honest. Like I said, he likes to keep to himself."

"I see. Well, that's a plus." I smiled. "Thank you for the tour. I'll be in touch if I feel this is the right boat for me."

"It was my pleasure." He nodded.

I walked around the marina for a bit trying to see if anyone else was out that I could talk to. No such luck, so I took an Uber back to the hotel to change and get ready for my dinner date with Mr. Pines. As I was touching up my hair with a few curls, my phone rang, and it was my mother calling.

"Hello," I answered against my better judgment.

"Laurel, darling. I haven't heard from you in a while."

"Sorry, Mom. I've been really busy. In fact, I'm in California right now working on a story."

"That's nice, dear. I was calling to tell you that Bella is the lead dancer in *Swan Lake* next weekend and we're all going.

The Interview: New York & Los Angeles

You need to be there to support your sister, Laurel."

Silence overtook me for a moment. I knew she was calling for a reason. God forbid she ever called just to see how I was doing.

"New York City, right?"

"Yes, that's right," she answered.

"It just so happens I have to be there for another story, so I'll be able to come and see Bella dance."

"Fabulous. I have tickets for Saturday night at eight o'clock. I'll text you the address."

"Sounds good, Mom. By the way, how's Dad?"

"Your father is your father, Laurel," she replied with a snippy tone.

I rolled my eyes. "Alrighty then, I'll see you in New York."

After I ended the call, I booked an Uber to pick me up at the hotel. Grabbing my purse, I headed down to the lobby and waited outside the doors. A few moments later, a black Ford Expedition pulled up to the curb.

Chapter Six

After climbing out of the Expedition, I walked down to Craig's boat.

"Knock, knock," I shouted.

"In the kitchen."

The smell that greeted me as I walked down the steps was amazing. I couldn't put my finger on what it was, but my belly started doing a happy dance.

"It smells delicious in here." I smiled as I found him by the stove.

"Thanks." He beamed as he turned around and our eyes met. "Wow. You look great."

"Thank you." I grinned. "I brought some wine." I held up a bottle of Pinot Grigio. "Is there anything I can help you with?"

"Nope. Everything is all set."

He opened the oven door and removed a pan from the rack. I couldn't help but stare at his fine ass as he bent over.

"I wanted to keep it simple because I wasn't too sure what you liked, so I made spaghetti with a homemade vodka sauce and clams, fresh garlic bread, and a kale salad with cucumbers, tomatoes, and homemade croutons tossed with a light lemon vinaigrette dressing."

The Interview: New York & Los Angeles

"It sounds delicious." I smiled.

He handed me the basket with the garlic bread in it and I followed him up to the deck where he had a round table covered with a white tablecloth, two candles burning in the middle, and fine china that sat on top.

"I'm going to grab the wine. Please, have a seat." He pulled out my chair for me.

"Such a gentleman." I smiled. "Thank you."

He was back in a flash with the wine and two wine glasses. After pouring our drinks, he took the seat across from me.

"Be honest with me, Craig. Why the boat?" I asked as I placed the linen napkin in my lap.

"Why not? It's just me. Plus, I like it here."

"Why? Because it's easy to isolate yourself from the rest of the world?"

He narrowed his eye at me as he took a bite of his spaghetti.

"What makes you think I do that?"

"You don't really have neighbors here, not many people to talk to, and you can sail off at any time. It's easy to live on this boat and not be bothered by anyone."

"Are you interviewing me, Miss Holloway?" He picked up his wine glass.

"No." I raised my brow.

"I'm a very busy man. I own a popular restaurant in which I am the chef just about every night, not to mention I take care of all the business stuff. I don't have the time to keep up with a house. And like I said, it's just me, so living on the boat is perfect."

"But don't you get lonely?" I asked as I took a sip of my wine.

"No. I choose this kind of life, Laurel. This is who I am."

"I get a feeling that this isn't who you were." I paused. "What happened to you, Mr. Pines?"

His gaze narrowed, and he got up from his seat and stood by the railing, staring out into the water.

"Life happened," he replied in a monotone voice.

I got up from my seat, grabbed his drink from the table, and walked over to him, placing his glass in his hand. He glanced over at me and I could see the sadness that resided in his eyes.

"I didn't ask you here to talk about this," he spoke.

In that moment, when I saw a hint of tears swell up, I knew tragedy had struck him. I could feel his pain and the heartache he'd been carrying around with him. I placed my hand on his cheek as our eyes locked onto each other's.

"You don't have to," I whispered.

He set his drink on the railing and brought his hand up to my forehead, brushing away a strand of my hair. His hand roamed down my cheek until it stopped, and he cupped my chin.

"You're a beautiful woman, Laurel," he softly spoke.

My lips formed a small smile as the raging ache down below intensified. Lowering his head, his lips softly brushed against mine. I welcomed his kiss and returned the favor. Soon our tongues met and tangled in the night air, leaving me breathless and wanting more.

"I hope you don't mind that I did that." He lightly smiled as he broke our kiss.

"I don't mind at all. In fact, I wouldn't mind if you kept

The Interview: New York & Los Angeles

going," I replied as my lips pressed against his.

He bent down, picked me up with his strong muscular arms, and carried me to his bedroom, where he gently laid me on his bed, our lips still locked together. The heat coursing through my veins and the skin that trembled under his fingers as they lightly roamed up my thigh was unbearable. I was hot for Craig Pines and I couldn't wait until he was buried deep inside me.

He broke our passionate kiss as his tongue slid across the flesh of my neck. My breath became bated as my heart pounded with excitement. He lifted himself off me and slowly took down the straps of my sundress, pulling it from my body and tossing it on the floor as he stood at the end of the bed and stared at me in nothing but my bra and panties. I sat up on my elbows and watched as he stripped out of his clothes and was left standing in nothing but his gray boxers. His body was solid. His abs were defined and the sexy V-line he sported was the best one I'd ever seen on any guy I'd ever slept with. I swallowed hard as he took down his boxers, revealing his perfect God-given package. He leaned over as his fingers gripped the sides of my panties and he slowly took them down, exposing my freshly shaven pussy that desperately wanted him. His tongue slid up my thigh, slowly and seductively, making its way up to my slick opening. Gripping the comforter, I arched my back and let out a pleasing moan as his mouth explored me from the inside out. His hands roamed up my sides until they met my breasts. Pulling my bra cups down, he took my hardened peaks between his thumbs and forefingers, delicately rubbing them and sending my body into overdrive. Several moans escaped me while his tongue slid up my torso and he let go of one breast and dipped his finger inside me.

"Oh my God." I threw my head back.

"Do you want more?" he spoke in a low voice.

"Yes. God, yes!" I exclaimed.

"Then you're going to have to come for me first."

"Trust me. Keep doing what you're doing and that won't be a problem."

He hovered over me with a smile and pressed his lips against mine. His finger continued to explore me while his thumb circled my clit, sending my body into one hell of an orgasm. While I was basking in the glory of the pleasure Craig gave me, he removed my bra, slipped on a condom, and before I knew it, he was inside me, moving in and out at a slow and steady pace. He rolled over onto his back and pulled me on top of him. I quickly sat up and rode his cock as if my life depended on it while his hands groped my breasts. The buildup was coming and bigger than the last one. His moans heightened as did mine while he placed his hands on my hips, holding me down and moaning while we both came at the same time. I was breathless as I collapsed on top of him and wrapped my arms around his neck. Once we both regained a normal heartrate and our breathing slowed, I rolled off him as he extended his arm and I snuggled into him.

"Wow." I smiled as my lips pressed against his firm and muscular chest.

He chuckled as he softly stroked my hair.

"Damn, Laurel. That was amazing. I'll be right back. Don't move." He lifted his arm and climbed out of bed to dispose of the condom.

He climbed back into bed, but not before grabbing our glasses and filling them with wine. As he handed me my drink, I sat up, covering myself with the sheet and taking the glass from his hand.

"Thank you." I smiled.

"You're welcome. When are you going back to Seattle?"

"I have a couple more days here," I spoke as I brought the glass up to my lips.

The Interview: New York & Los Angeles

"Good. I was thinking that maybe you'd want to take the boat out with me tomorrow."

"I'd like that." I bashfully smiled. "I thought you didn't bring women on your boat."

"Like I said before, I normally don't. But there have been a couple who have been here over the past years."

"Girlfriends?" I arched my brow.

"It wasn't anything but sex," he replied.

"I like your style, Mr. Pines." I grinned.

"Let me ask you something, Laurel." His eye narrowed at me.

"Ask away." I took a sip of my wine.

"Why are you single?"

"Who says I am?" I smirked.

"I hope to God you're joking because we just had sex and I don't have sex with women who are in relationships."

"Relax. I'm not in a relationship."

"So, I'll ask you again. Why is a woman like you single?"

Chapter Seven

He was just as curious as to why I was single as I was to his reasons.

"Tell me why you're single first and then I'll tell you why I am," I spoke.

He sighed as he grabbed the wine bottle from the nightstand and refilled my glass.

"I'm single because I choose to be, and that's all you need to know."

"Okay, then. Me too."

"See, the difference is that what you tell me will stay in this bedroom. What I tell you will end up in an article that millions of people will read."

"I already told you that the article will be a day in the life. I won't write anything personal," I spoke. "Don't you trust me?"

"I don't know you very well, Laurel," he spoke in a serious tone. "So, I can't really answer that."

"You certainly didn't feel that way when you just fucked me," I spoke with irritation.

I threw back the covers, and as I started to climb out of bed, Craig grabbed my hand with a firm grip.

The Interview: New York & Los Angeles

"Don't," he spoke in a firm tone. "You need to understand where I'm coming from. You came here, to me, to get an interview on why I'm still single. Do you think just because we had sex I forgot about that?"

"No," I softly spoke.

"Did you have sex with me hoping to get a story?" he asked as he let go of my hand.

"Of course not. I had sex with you because you're hot and I was horny. It's what I do. I have casual sex all the time. No strings, no emotions, nothing. Just sex."

"Then we're not so different," he spoke. "You obviously have your reasons and so do I. Let's leave it at that. Now climb back in here." He held out his arm.

"I really should get back to the hotel. I'll need a change of clothes for tomorrow."

"I'll tell you what. I'll drive you back and you can pack a small bag. Then we'll come back here and set sail first thing tomorrow morning."

"Are you sure?" I asked.

"Yes." He smiled.

"Why aren't you working tomorrow?" I narrowed my eye at him.

"You wanted a day in the life, so I'm giving it to you. Besides spending a majority of my time at the restaurant, I like to spend what little free days I have on the water."

We both got dressed and headed to the hotel. After packing my swimsuit and a change of clothes, we went back to Craig's boat where we had round two of sex and then drifted off into a relaxing sleep. Well, he did. It took me a while because I couldn't stop thinking about how he told me "life happened." I needed to know the story behind that, and I was going to find out one way or another.

The next morning, I awoke, and when I rolled over, my arm hit the empty spot next to me. Opening my eyes, I noticed Craig wasn't there. I climbed out of bed, slipped into my short black satin robe, and headed to the kitchen area, where I could smell the aroma of fresh brewed coffee and food cooking.

"Good morning." Craig smiled as he turned and looked at me.

"Good morning. What is that wonderful smell besides fresh brewed coffee?"

"I'm making us some breakfast before we head out. I hope you like eggs benedict."

"I do. It's one of my favorite breakfast foods." I grinned.

"Help yourself to some coffee while I plate this."

I walked over to the coffee pot and poured myself a cup, leaning against the counter and sipping it while I stared at how sexy Craig was plating our breakfast. I could hear my phone ringing from my purse, so I walked over and pulled it out, noticing it was George calling.

"Hello, handsome," I answered, and Craig glanced over at me.

"Hello, sunshine. How's Cali treating you?"

"Very well, thank you. What's up?"

"Not much. Just checking in to see how the interview is going. Eric told me you needed a couple of extra days."

"Oh, you know."

"You can't talk, can you?"

"Not right now. I'm a little busy. Mr. Pines and I are just

The Interview: New York & Los Angeles

about to have breakfast."

"You slept with him?"

"That would be a yes from me. So, I'll talk to you soon. Love you."

"I want every last delicious detail! You better call me when you're free."

"Will do." I ended the call.

"May I ask who you're calling handsome?" Craig's brow arched as he set our plates down on the table.

"That was my best friend George." I smiled as I took a seat.

"Your best friend is a guy?"

"Yes." I smiled as I picked up my fork.

"Is he gay or something?" he asked.

"No. He has a girlfriend. Why?"

"Just curious. How long have the two of you known each other?"

"Since college. He was there for me when I caught my best friend and my boyfriend at the time fucking in my dorm room. We met in the parking lot when I was loading some boxes in my car."

"And the two of you never—"

"Had sex? No. We're best friends and that's it. He's like a brother to me. So, if we did have sex, that would just be weird." I smirked.

"You're single because you don't trust men. Am I right?" he asked.

"You're partially right. By the way, this is delicious. I could totally get used to this."

Craig let out a chuckle. "Thank you. I'm happy you're enjoying it. I'm only partially right?"

"Yes. I don't trust men and you can thank my father for that." I pointed at him with my fork.

"Why?" He gave me a confused look.

"I already told you he cheats on my mother," I spoke as I picked up my coffee cup.

"And you also told me that your mother sleeps with the pool boy." He smirked.

"True. But, in her defense, she does it because my father is too busy with work and fucking his secretaries to give her any attention."

"So, she knows he cheats?" His brow raised.

"Yep. But he doesn't know she knows."

"Am I to assume he doesn't know about the pool boy either?" he asked.

"No. He doesn't. Actually, it's just the pool boy in the summer, but her tennis coach all year round."

"Oh. Okay, then." He smirked before taking a sip of his coffee.

"I told you my family was dysfunctional."

I got up from the table, grabbed our empty plates, and took them over to the sink.

"So, what's the other reason you're single?" he asked.

"I don't believe that relationships can ever last. Eventually, everything fades away."

The Interview: New York & Los Angeles

"Your parents are still married."

"Right. And look at how they behave. It's disgusting."

"I don't understand why they don't get divorced," Craig spoke as he helped me wash the dishes.

"Because there's too much at stake. Too much money and too many properties. Neither one of them love each other anymore, but they're too damn selfish to do anything about it. Plus, they love being known as Boston's most influential and perfect couple."

"What about your siblings? How do they feel?"

"Alfie is following right into my dad's shoes and Bella is off in her own world with her dancing. The three of us never really talked about it. My dad is Alfie's hero and Bella acts like nothing's wrong."

Craig finished drying the last dish and set the towel neatly on the counter.

"Shall we set sail?" He smiled.

"Let's go." I grinned.

Chapter Eight

It was a beautiful day; calm, clear, and picturesque. I stood on the deck with my hands planted on the railing, staring out at the vast blue ocean water.

"I can see why your best friend is a guy," Craig spoke as he walked up next to me.

"Why is that?" I turned to him with a smile as he rested his elbows against the rail.

"You're easy to talk to, and sometimes a guy needs someone of the opposite sex to tell things that he can't tell his male friends because they wouldn't understand."

"Like what?" I asked in confusion.

"There's this woman that comes into the restaurant every Saturday and Sunday night. She makes a reservation and asks to be seated at the same table for two. She's been doing it for months."

"Do you know why?"

"I haven't got a clue." He sighed.

"Why are you telling me this?"

"I'm not sure." He turned his head and looked at me.

"Is she pretty?"

The Interview: New York & Los Angeles

"She's very pretty."

I nudged his shoulder with mine.

"Why don't you talk to her?"

"Nah. I can't." He gave a small smile.

"Sure, you can. It's easy. You talk to me."

"You really don't give me a choice. Do you?" A smirk crossed his lips.

"No. I guess I don't." I smiled. "What's her name?"

"Maddy. I only know that because I was up at the hostess desk one night when she walked in."

"And no one's ever met her for dinner?"

"No. She always eats alone. How about taking the jet ski out?" he asked as he abruptly changed the subject.

"Sounds fun. Let's do it." I grinned.

Something told me that Craig had a special interest in this Maddy woman but was too afraid for one reason or another to talk to her. Mental note to myself, *find out what Craig Pines is hiding.*

He climbed on the jet ski first, then I took my place behind him, wrapping my arms securely around his waist. We took off, flying across the water as the wind swept over our faces. Sheer terror overtook me for a moment as he sped up and the sting in my eyes from the saltwater nearly blinded me. Why the hell didn't I listen to him when he told me to wear my sunglasses? That's right, I was afraid of them flying off my face. I'd spent $300 on those couture sunglasses that framed my face to perfection and I wasn't about to let them sink down to the bottom of the ocean.

"You okay?" he yelled back at me with the slight turn of his head.

"I'm fine."

Fine if you love your pelvis banging against the damn seat to the point where sex could potentially be out of the question.

"Hold on tight," he spoke as he made a sharp turn, tipping the jet ski on its side.

I held on for dear life and said a couple prayers in case this was the moment I would die. He slowed down as we approached the boat. I wasn't a very religious person, but once the jet ski came to a complete standstill, I made the sign of the cross and let out a deep breath. I climbed off and onto the deck, collapsing into the chair on the sundeck. Craig stood over me as he dried himself off with a towel and a smirk across his face.

"Isn't it the best feeling in the world?" he asked.

"It sure is. It doesn't get any better than knowing you're on the verge of death," I sarcastically spoke.

He chuckled as he took the seat next to me.

"How about you come to the restaurant for dinner tomorrow night. I won't be able to see you until then. I have something to do in the morning." His voice lowered as he stared out into the water.

There was something that told me whatever it was he had to do, it was personal, and he didn't want me knowing, which piqued my curiosity even more. The more time I spent with Craig Pines, the more mysterious he became.

The day on the open water was well spent, and when it was time to dock, it was time for me to head back to the hotel. As much as my bruised and aching pelvis wanted to stay, I couldn't. I had to work on Everything Laurel and get it in to Eric by tomorrow morning or his face would be plastered all over my phone and his voice would penetrate my ears.

The Interview: New York & Los Angeles

"I know you have to go. Let me drop you off. I'm going to head over to the restaurant and check up on things."

"I'm sure they're doing fine without you." I grinned as I poked his chest. "But you can still drive me to my hotel."

When Craig pulled up to the Four Seasons, I reached over and placed my hand on his.

"Thanks for today. It was a lot of fun." I smiled.

"You're welcome. I'll put your name down for tomorrow night at six o'clock."

"I'll see you then."

I gave him a tender smile as I opened the door and headed into the lobby. As I exited the elevator and walked down the hallway to my room, my phone rang, and Eric's lovely face appeared on the screen. Rolling my eyes, I answered it.

"What's up, Eric?" I smiled as I swiped the keycard to my room.

"What's going on with Everything Laurel? Why don't I have it in my inbox? I need what you have to submit by Monday."

"Calm down. It's almost done. I'm finishing it now."

"Really, because it looks like you just got back from someplace." His brows furrowed.

"I was with Craig."

"I hope you got the interview because you need to move on. You've been in California too long already."

"I've only been here two days. Relax. I'm getting it. I'm in for the rest of the night, and as soon as I finish up Everything Laurel, I'm working on the article."

"So why is the guy still single?" he asked.

57

Shit. Why did he have to put me on the spot?

"Because he hasn't found the right woman yet. It happens, Eric. He's picky."

"I need more than that." He pointed at me.

I rolled my eyes and sighed.

"I have to go. I need to order room service and get to work."

"You better not order anything expensive!"

"Bye, Eric." I grinned as I ended the call.

After I took a relaxing bath, I slipped into the comfy white robe provided by the hotel, climbed on the bed, and placed an order for room service, which included a bottle of wine. My intuition was still bothering me about Craig's plans for tomorrow morning and my mind wouldn't rest until I knew exactly what he was doing. Picking up the phone, I called room service back.

"Hi, this is Laurel Holloway. I need to cancel my room service. Something has come up and I need to step out."

"Very well, Miss Holloway. If there's anything you need, don't hesitate to call."

"Thank you."

I changed out of my robe and into a coral sundress that was labeled as dressy casual. After slipping my feet into a low-heeled sandal, I headed across to Rosie's.

"May I help you?" the perky brunette smiled.

"Dinner for one."

"Do you have a reservation?"

"I'm afraid I don't."

The Interview: New York & Los Angeles

"I'm sorry, but we're all booked up for the evening," she spoke.

I turned my head and looked around to see if I could horn in on someone's table. Damn it. No one.

"May I sit at the bar and have a drink at least?"

"If you can find a seat. It looks pretty packed."

"Thanks. I'll give it a shot." I grinned.

Walking over to the bar, I found that every seat was taken. I sighed as I plotted my next move. That was when I spotted a gentleman getting up and he laid his suitcoat across the stool. I waited until he was out of sight and then walked over, picked up his jacket, and took a seat.

"Hey, Laurel." Barney smiled. "Someone is sitting there. He just ran to the restroom."

"Oh well." I smiled. "I didn't realize. I'm here now, so he'll have to find somewhere else to sit."

Barney lightly shook his head.

"Neat martini, straight up with two olives?" he asked.

"You remembered." I grinned.

"Coming right up."

"Excuse me, but you're in my seat."

"I am?" I cocked my head.

"Yes, you are," he spoke in a stern voice.

"Then this must be yours?" I held up his suitcoat. "I thought someone left it."

"I left it there on purpose, so no one would take my seat."

59

"I see. I'm Laurel." I extended my hand. "And you are?"

"Joe." He dismissed my hand.

"Let me ask you something, Joe. Are you married or dating anyone?"

"No. I'm not, and why are you asking?" he spoke with irritation.

"Because I can see why." I smiled. "A man not giving up his seat for a woman says a lot about his character."

"Who the hell do you think you are, lady?" he snapped.

"What's going on here? Laurel, what are you doing?" Craig asked as he walked up.

"This lady purposely took my seat while I was in the restroom."

Craig lightly grabbed my martini and my arm.

"I apologize, sir. Laurel, come with me."

"You ruined all my fun." I smirked. "I was in the middle of telling him what a gentleman he was not."

"What are you doing here?"

"Well, I was hungry, and I wanted to ask you something."

"I thought you had work to do."

"I do, but I can't concentrate on an empty stomach, and your food is so good," I whined.

He looked around the restaurant for a moment and then led me to a table that was being cleaned up.

"You can sit here."

"Excuse me, Mr. Pines, I was just going to seat someone here

The Interview: New York & Los Angeles

that has reservations," the not-so-perky brunette spoke.

"They'll have to wait. Miss Holloway is sitting here now. Give them my apologies and tell them dinner is on me tonight."

The not-so-perky brunette glared at me as she walked away.

"Thank you." I smiled at Craig.

I noticed his eyes diverting behind me. I couldn't very well turn around or else it would be obvious, so I'd wait until he left.

"What do you want to eat?" he asked.

"Surprise me." I smiled.

"Fine, and when I bring it over, we can talk for a minute. It's really busy, Laurel."

"I thought you were only here to check up on things." I narrowed my eye.

"I am." He winked.

Chapter Nine

When Craig escorted me to the table, I hung my purse on the back of the chair. After he walked away, I discreetly knocked it onto the floor. Reaching back, I looked at the table behind me only to notice a woman with long brown hair and brown eyes sitting alone. That must be the woman he told me about. She was definitely pretty, and I could see why Craig was attracted to her, even though he wouldn't admit it.

"Here's your salad," Craig spoke as he set it down in front of me.

"Thank you." I smiled as I placed my napkin in my lap. "I have to say that having the owner serve me himself is quite a treat."

"Your food should be up shortly," he spoke as he glanced behind me.

"I love the suspense of not knowing what I'll be eating."

He gave me a small smile and walked away. I was going to have to find out what the hell was going on with this woman. My journalist instincts were at an all-time high. I decided to switch chairs and face her, for which I was going to have to come up with some explanation as to why I did when Craig came back.

As I ate my salad, I discreetly glanced at her from time to time. There was a sadness about her. That much I could tell, just

The Interview: New York & Los Angeles

by the way she sat in her seat and slowly picked at her food.

"Why did you switch seats?" Craig asked as he brought over my plate of food and set it down in front of me.

"Because I'm in clear view of that snooty little hostess of yours and she keeps looking at me," I lied as I arched my brow. "It's making me uncomfortable. Anyway, what do we have here?" I grinned.

"Parmesan-crusted organic chicken with asparagus topped with basil and lemon butter and roasted sweet potatoes," he spoke as he took the seat next to me, so he could still get a view of the sad-looking woman. "What did you want to ask me?"

"Well," I spoke as I picked up my fork and knife. "I was thinking that maybe I could tag along with you tomorrow morning to wherever it is you're going, to complete a day in the life."

"No, Laurel. I'm sorry. I'm doing something personal tomorrow and I don't want any company. I hope you understand."

"Sure, off course I do," I lied with an understanding tone. "I just thought I'd ask."

His eyes diverted more than once to the table where Maddy sat. I wanted so badly to say something, but not yet. He said she came on Sundays as well, which meant I would have to devise a plan before tomorrow night.

"This is incredible, Craig. Thank you." I softly smiled.

"You're welcome. I need to get back in the kitchen. I'll see you tomorrow evening."

"See you then."

He walked away, and I watched as Maddy got up and headed towards the restroom. After waiting a moment, I got up from my seat and followed her. I stood at the sink and let the warm water run over my hands while I waited for her to come out of the stall. This wasn't creepy, right? Not in the least. I heard the toilet flush, and when she emerged from the stall, she walked over to the sink next to me. I looked up in the mirror and gave her a small smile. She returned the favor.

"I love this restaurant," I spoke as I dried my hands and then reached in my purse for my lip gloss. "The food here is so amazing."

"It's nice." She softly smiled. "And the food is really good," she spoke as she grabbed a piece of paper towel and dried off her hands.

I opened the door and held it for her.

"Thank you."

"No problem."

We both went back to our tables. I took my seat and signaled for the waitress to bring me my check.

"Mr. Pines said dinner was on him tonight." She smiled.

"Well, isn't he a sweet man." I grinned. "Thank you."

"Have a good night, Miss Holloway."

I fumbled in my purse and took out my ringing phone, noticing that George was calling.

"Hello," I answered.

"What's up, buttercup? Staying out of trouble?"

Maddy inserted some cash into the leather billfold and got up from her seat.

"Yeah. As much as I can."

"Uh oh. I know that tone. What's going on?"

The Interview: New York & Los Angeles

I got up from my seat, and when I left the restaurant, I saw her drive away in a silver Mercedes.

"I'm just heading back to the hotel to finish up Everything Laurel, so Eric will get off my back."

"So how did you end up having sex with Mr. Pines? Are you tripping into some feelings?" he asked.

"No, I'm not tripping into some feelings. He's sexy, great in bed, and a sweet guy. If I totally wanted to have feelings, I would in a second. He's hiding something, George."

"Like what? What do you mean?"

"I'm not sure, but I'll find out tomorrow morning. There's a specific reason why he won't let anyone get close to him. I've asked around, but nobody seems to know anything about him."

"That's strange."

"That's why I need a couple of more days."

"Okay. Keep me posted. Veronica says hi."

"Tell her I said hi and that we need to go shopping once I get back."

"Will do. Talk to you later, Laurel."

"Bye, George."

Once I was back in my room, I set my purse down on the table, grabbed my laptop, and took it out to the balcony to get some work done.

****

The next morning, I woke up at the crack of dawn and had the hotel call me a cab since there didn't seem to be any Uber's available. We waited at the entrance of the marina for Craig's car to pull out.

"Lady, what are we doing?" the cab driver asked.

"We're waiting for someone."

"And how long is this going to take?" he asked with irritation.

"What does it matter? The meter is running, and you'll get paid. By the way, my name is Laurel." I smiled. "What's yours?"

"George."

"Oh, my best friend's name is George."

"And?"

"I was just saying," I spoke as I sipped my coffee.

About an hour later, Craig's called pulled out of the marina.

"See that black car that just pulled out?"

"Yeah."

"Follow it, but don't let him see you."

"Are you doing something illegal, lady?" he asked. "Because if you are, I don't want to be involved."

"Is following someone illegal?" I arched my browed.

"It is considered a form of stalking."

I waved my hand in front of my face.

"Well, we aren't stalking him. In fact, he's a friend of mine, and I just want to see where he's going since he wouldn't tell me."

"Maybe he's seeing some other chick."

"I can guarantee he's not."

The Interview: New York & Los Angeles

"You never know. You may not like what you're about to find out," he spoke.

"Just follow him and be discreet about it."

George, the cab driver, followed Craig until we reached the cemetery.

"Do you want me to follow him in there?" he asked.

"No. He'll know. I'm going to get out here. Wait for me."

I opened the door and climbed out. Upon entering the cemetery, I saw Craig's car pulled along the curb several feet in front of me. Like the crazy person I was, I hid behind a tall gravestone that belonged to a Mr. Alexander Bentley.

"Sorry, Mr. Bentley, but I need to use you for a moment," I whispered.

Why was he here? Stupid question. People come to the cemetery to visit their loved ones. Maybe his mom? His grandma? His dad? Perhaps a sibling? I wasn't sure because the subject of Craig's family never came up. But why would he keep coming to the cemetery a secret from me? This didn't make sense.

I stood there and watched him as he held two bouquets of red roses and set them down on the graves. It had to be his parents. Maybe this was something he did once a month or perhaps every Sunday. But still the lingering question wouldn't stop haunting me. *Why wouldn't he tell me?*

He took a seat on the grass and sat there for about an hour before climbing back in his car and driving away. I sighed as I stood up straight and felt a cramp in my leg. Once I saw he was completely out of the cemetery, I walked over to where the graves were he visited and read the engraved gravestones.

Here lies Rebecca Grace Pines, beloved wife, daughter, and friend.

My heart started racing as I read the second one.

Here lies Rosie Jennifer Pines, beloved daughter of Craig & Rebecca Pines. With the date engraved as 2013-2013.

I swallowed hard as my heart broke in two. This wasn't his parents' grave. It was his wife and daughter's. A sickness fell over me as I sank down into the luscious green grass and stared at their graves.

"Hey, Laurel, you okay?" George the cab driver asked as he approached me from behind. "I saw him leave, so I pulled in."

"He had a wife and daughter," I softly spoke.

"You're his friend and didn't know that?" he asked.

"No." I shook my head.

I got up from the grass and slowly walked back to the cab.

"Back to the Four Seasons, please," I spoke.

"Yeah. Sure thing, Laurel."

I sat in the back of the cab all the way to the hotel and didn't say a word. His wife and daughter must have been the reason he closed himself off to anyone. *Shit.* Could I blame him? I paid George the enormous cab fare that Eric was going to kill me for and went up to my room. Craig didn't open his restaurant until 2014, a year after his wife and daughter passed. Rosie's. He named the restaurant after his daughter. Chills ran through me. I was a tough cookie, but this, this was getting to me. As I was in deep thought, Eric's face appeared on my phone.

"Hey," I answered in a somber tone.

"What's wrong, Laurel? You look upset."

"Nothing, Eric. What's up?"

"Thanks for getting Everything Laurel to me. It looks good.

The Interview: New York & Los Angeles

Have you gotten any pictures yet of Mr. Pines for the article?"

"Not yet. I'll get them before I leave."

"And when is that? Your time is expiring."

"I know, Eric," I spoke with irritation. "A couple of days. By the way, I'm going to take a couple personal days in New York either before or after I snag an interview with Wyatt Coleman. My sister is dancing in *Swan Lake* as the lead and I promised my parents I would attend. It's next Saturday."

"You're paying for that on your own dime, Laurel. The company isn't paying for you to gallivant around New York on personal business."

"Yeah. That's fine. Don't worry about it."

"Are you sure everything's okay? You're acting weird and I don't like it. Have you fallen for Craig Pines?"

"No. I started my period and I'm in a funk. Hormones, you know."

He put his hand up.

"TMI, Laurel."

"You asked." I raised my brow.

"Finish up there and get out. You still have Wyatt Coleman to interview."

"I know. Bye, Eric." I kissed the screen and ended the call.

Chapter Ten

Grabbing my laptop, I sat on the bed with my legs extended and my back up against the headboard. In the Google search bar, I typed: *Rebecca Pines*. Instantly, an article popped up with her name highlighted, so I clicked it and sat there in shock as I read what it had to say. My heart ached, and I couldn't bring myself to read any further.

It was almost six o'clock, so I left the hotel and walked to Rosie's. When I arrived, the same snooty hostess from last night was standing behind the counter.

"Hello." I smiled. "Reservation for Laurel Holloway."

"Right this way, Miss Holloway," she spoke as she grabbed a menu and led me over to the same table I was at last night. Was this a coincidence?

"Your server will be right with you." She pleasantly smiled as she handed me my menu.

"Thank you."

After setting my purse down and rearranging the perfectly folded napkin that housed the silverware (a bad habit of mine), I looked up and saw Maddy take a seat at the same table as last night.

"Hello there." Craig smiled as he walked over to me.

The Interview: New York & Los Angeles

"Hey. It's good to see you." I grinned.

"Good to see you too." His eyes diverted over to Maddy.

"Go talk to her, Craig." I placed my hand on him arm.

"Laurel, no. Stop. You don't know what you're talking about."

"I know who she is. She was here last night, same table."

"I have to get back into the kitchen," he nervously spoke as he walked away.

I took in a deep breath, grabbed my menu, and walked over to Maddy's table.

"Excuse me. Hi." I smiled. "We met last night in the bathroom."

"Oh. Yes. Hi."

"Do you mind if I join you?" I took the seat across from her before she had time to answer.

"Umm. I don't—"

"Thanks." I grinned.

I spotted the snotty hostess and waved her over.

"Yes?"

"You can go ahead and seat someone at my table. I'm going to join," I glanced at Maddy, "Maddy. My friend Maddy for dinner."

"Oh. Okay. Sure." She smiled in delight and walked away.

"It's really no fun to eat alone. You must really love this place to be back here for the second night in a row."

"I can say the same for you," she spoke.

"Oh. I'm just here visiting. I'm from Seattle. By the way, I'm Laurel."

"What brings you to Los Angeles?" she asked.

"Business. I work for the *Seattle Times*, and I write a column called Everything Laurel."

"Oh my gosh." She perked up. "I've read that a few times. In fact, your columns came up when I was looking something up online."

"Oh." I smiled. "What do you think?" I leaned across the table. "It's okay if you think I suck."

She let out a light laugh.

"No. I think your columns are great. You give good advice."

"Thank you." I placed the napkin on my lap.

The waitress walked over, took our dinner order, and then proceeded to tell me that I was wanted in the kitchen.

"Excuse me, Maddy. I'll be right back."

I walked into the kitchen and found Craig standing there with his arms folded and a scowl across his face.

"You wanted to see me?" My brow arched.

"What the hell do you think you're doing?" he asked in a stern voice. "Why are you sitting at Maddy's table?"

"I'm a journalist, Craig. You wanted to know why she comes to your restaurant every Saturday and Sunday at the same time and sits at the same table. Well, I'm going to find out for you."

"Laurel, this isn't funny. Get back to your table."

"No can do, Mr. Pines. Someone is already sitting there. Now you need to relax." I placed my hand on his chest. "And by the way, can you please make my and Maddy's food a top

The Interview: New York & Los Angeles

priority? I'm starving." I smirked as I walked out of his kitchen.

"Everything okay?" Maddy asked.

"Oh yeah." I waved my hand in front of my face. "I'm doing a day in the life of the owner of this restaurant and he had a question for me. The *Seattle Times* is branching out and created a magazine called *Fusion Daily*. My boss put me in charge of interviewing successful, rich, and handsome men under the age of thirty-five."

"Wow. I want your job." She lightly smiled.

"I know, right? It's tough, but someone's got to do it." I winked. "What do you do?" I asked her.

"I'm a fashion designer. My dream was to open an online store called Madison's Utopia." She looked down.

"Was?" I cocked my head.

"My husband passed away a year ago and I guess you could say that I've lost that dream. He was a big part of it, and when he died, that part of me died with him."

"I'm sorry, Maddy." I reached over and placed my hand on hers.

"Thanks. So am I." Her voice saddened. "We were only married two years." She let out a light laugh as she wiped her teary eyes. "I don't know why I'm telling you this. I don't ever talk about it with anyone, not even my family."

"Well, I've been told many times that I'm a very easy person to talk to."

"Yeah. You are." She picked up her wine glass.

"So why are you back tonight if you had dinner here last night?"

"I've been coming here every Saturday and Sunday night for

months and I sit at this table. My husband held business meetings here and raved about the food and the view. He wanted to take me here so badly because he knew I'd love it. So, for our anniversary, he made reservations and asked if we could be seated at this table because it had the best view. He passed away two days before our anniversary. Coming here helps me feel close to him. The weekends were our time together. No business, no calls, nothing. Just the two of us."

Oh my God, my heart was breaking for her. The waitress walked over and set our plates down in front of us.

"Thank you. Could you please ask Mr. Pines to come out here for a moment? I need a word with him." I smiled.

"Sure. I'll send him out."

A few moments later, our waitress returned.

"I'm sorry, Miss Holloway, but Mr. Pines is really busy and can't leave the kitchen."

"Okay. Well, thank you anyway."

I knew damn well he wasn't that busy. He was just afraid to come out and show himself because of Maddy.

"Is the owner the one who was at your table last night?" she asked.

"Yes." My eyes lit up. "He's so handsome, isn't he?" I grinned.

"He is. I've seen him a lot. Is he also the chef?"

"He is." My eyes widened. "That's why the food here is so spectacular."

"I'd love to meet him. My husband just raved so much about this place and the food. I would like to thank him."

"Then you shall." I smiled.

The Interview: New York & Los Angeles

We continued talking while we ate. Once we were finished, I took care of the bill.

"Seriously, Laurel. Let me pay for mine."

"Nah." I waved my hand. "My boss is paying. We talked business."

"We did?" She gave me a confused look.

"Of course. We talked about Madison's Utopia. In fact, once you get that online store opened, I want to feature it in our magazine."

"Are you serious, Laurel?"

"Yes, I'm very serious. I'll do an interview with you and help spread the word." I smiled.

"I don't know what to say. Thank you so much." Tears sprang to her eyes.

"You're welcome. Now all I need you to do is go after your dream."

Her lips formed a smile as she gently squeezed my hand.

"In fact, give me your number so we can keep in touch," I spoke as I pulled out my phone.

After she rattled her number off, she left the restaurant, and I took a seat at the bar until Craig was finished working.

"Still here, Laurel?" Barney smiled.

"I'm waiting for Craig."

"He already left."

"What?" I narrowed my eye at him.

"He left about an hour ago."

"Ugh! Thanks, Barney."

Now I was angry. Why the fuck did he leave without saying anything? I stomped out of the restaurant, and luckily, there was a line of cabs waiting at the curb. Climbing in the back of one, I gave the cab driver Craig's address. When he pulled up to the marina, I walked down to his boat and saw him sitting on the deck with a drink in his hand.

"Nice of you to tell me you were leaving," I spoke in an irritated tone.

"I don't owe you any type of explanation." He took a sip of his drink.

"No, you don't, but it was rude, considering—"

"Considering what, Laurel?" he snapped. "You think I owe you because we slept together a few times?!"

"Do you not know me by now? I could care less if we had sex. That's not what I'm talking about. I thought we were friends."

"So, did I until you went and talked with Maddy. How could you do that?"

"Because I know you feel something for her."

"How the fuck can I when I don't even know her?" he shouted and walked down to the living area.

"She wants to meet you." I followed behind.

He stopped dead in his tracks and slowly turned around.

"What the hell did you say about me?"

"I told her why I was here. To follow you around for an article. Her husband passed away a year ago and your restaurant was his favorite. He made reservations for their anniversary because he wanted to take her there so bad, but he died two days before that could happen. She wants to meet the man who made her husband happy and excited to take her somewhere he loved."

He took a seat on the couch and placed his face in his hands.

"That's why she goes to Rosie's every Saturday and Sunday. It helps her feel close to him. I know you know what that feels like."

He slowly lifted his head and looked up at me.

"You don't know what you're talking about."

Chapter Eleven

His eyes narrowed at me as he spoke, and I could see the anger as plain as day. Not just anger, but sadness as well.

"I followed you this morning to the cemetery."

"You what?" he snapped as he stood up.

"I know about your wife and daughter and I'm sorry."

"Who the fuck do you think you are invading my privacy like that?" he yelled.

"Someone who cares about you and doesn't want to see you lock your life away because you're scared to love someone again."

"Look who the hell is talking!" he scowled. "Isn't the whole reason you stay away from relationships is because you're scared of getting hurt? Well, let me tell you something, Laurel, cheating is nothing compared to the pain of losing someone to death."

"I know that, Craig."

"Obviously, you don't. Get the hell out of here now!" He pointed at me. "I don't ever want to see you again. Do you understand me?!"

"Fine. I'll go. But let me ask you this. Is this what Rebecca would have wanted? Would she have wanted you to shut down and spend the rest of your life alone? Would you have wanted that for her? Think about that. I know it hurts, but it's time you started to heal. It's been five years. You still have your whole damn life in front of you. Don't waste it, because in the end, you'll only end up disappointing her, and I know you don't want to do that."

I turned and walked away. Once I was outside, I let out a deep breath as tears filled my eyes. I walked to the entrance of the marina and called an Uber to come get me. Once I was inside my hotel room, I combed the internet for a picture of Craig. Eric was going to kill me, but I didn't care. Fuck him for sending me here.

I poured myself a glass of wine and took it and the bottle out to the balcony. I stood over the railing with the glass pressed to my lips as if it was stuck. Suddenly, I heard a knock at the door. I walked back inside the room and opened it to find Craig standing there.

"Can I come in?" he asked.

"Depends. Are you going to yell at me again?" I raised my brow.

"No. I want to apologize to you."

"Then by all means, come in. Can I pour you a glass of wine?"

"No. I'm fine. Thanks."

His hands were tucked tightly into his pants pockets as he paced around the room.

"My father died when I was seven years old and my mother worked afternoons as a nurse in the ER. I was left with a babysitter who cared more about watching reruns of old TV shows than paying attention to me. My mother left it up to her to make sure I had dinner, and the best she could do was make me a peanut butter and jelly sandwich every night. Eventually,

I grew tired of it and decided to cook my own meals. I would sit in my room and watch cooking shows over and over again. I collected a folder filled with recipes and gave my mother a list of ingredients to buy when she went to the grocery store. It became an obsession. I loved preparing food that I knew would make people happy. It was then that I dreamed of owning my own restaurant. As soon as I was old enough, I worked in as many different ones as I could, learning the ropes, so to speak. I studied, and I watched. Sometimes, the chefs would let me help out in the kitchen and were amazed by the dishes I prepared, even though half the time, I was only a busboy. I studied abroad for two years in Paris and Italy, learning from some of the top chefs. After I graduated and returned home, I met Rebecca. I knew the moment I saw her that I was in love with her."

He took a seat on the couch in the living area and folded his hands while his elbows rested on his knees.

"We dated for three years before I proposed. There was no doubt in my mind that I wanted to spend the rest of my life with her. We married a year later. I was promoted to executive chef at a restaurant in San Francisco called Coi, and shortly after, the restaurant earned its first Michelin award. She shared my dream of opening up a restaurant and supported me one hundred percent. When we found out a couple of years later that she was pregnant, she decided that it was time I pursued my dream. I was skeptical at first because of our finances, and with a baby on the way, I thought it would be best to wait a couple of years. But she wouldn't have it. She said we'd be fine and she knew in her heart it was the right time. It took us seven months to find the perfect building, and two days before I was scheduled to close on the loan, I got the call. She was shopping at the mall with her girlfriend and they were having lunch in one of the restaurants when a man walked in with a gun looking for one of the waitresses. Rebecca was a therapist, and she calmed him down, but when the waitress he was looking for refused to come out and see him, he snapped and started shooting. He shot and killed three people, including Rebecca."

The Interview: New York & Los Angeles

Tears streamed down my face as I took a seat next to him and tightly grabbed his hand.

"She died instantly. The doctors at the hospital tried to save Rosie, but she died a couple of hours later."

"Craig, I'm so sorry."

He turned his head and his tear-filled eyes stared into mine.

"The day my wife and daughter died was the day I died with them. I couldn't stay in San Francisco after that. The memories were too haunting. A week later, I had their bodies transferred to the cemetery here and moved to Los Angeles. Six months later, I opened Rosie's. We knew we were having a girl and that was Rebecca's favorite name. I also knew that opening the restaurant was going to take every second of my time and I needed that distraction, so I put all my blood, sweat, and tears into making it the success it is today. The first year we were open, I won the Michelin Award. The restaurant was busy already, but after that, people started pouring in from all over the country, and soon enough, we were running out of space. So, when the building next door became vacant, I expanded, and my business grew even bigger. I literally became a success overnight. There are only a couple of people who know my story and that's the way I want to keep it."

"I understand," I softly spoke.

"You wanted to know why I'm single and that's the reason. I don't think I could ever love anyone as much as I loved Rebecca, and if by chance I did, I'd feel like I was betraying her in some way."

"You wouldn't be betraying her, Craig. She wouldn't want you to live the rest of your life alone."

"The moment Maddy walked into my restaurant, I could see and sense her sadness. The way she sat at the table and stared out the window. The way she slowly ate her food. I don't know, Laurel, I felt something, and it fucking freaked me out."

"You felt the same pain in her as you have," I softly spoke.

"Anyway, I'm sorry that I yelled at you the way I did. It wasn't fair to you."

"It's okay, Craig. Maybe I overstepped."

"Maybe?" He let out a light laugh.

"Okay, so I did, and for that, I'm sorry."

"It's fine, Laurel. You were only looking out for me. For what it's worth, I'm happy you were so damn pushy about following me around. If you weren't, we never would have become friends, and I want you as a friend. In fact, I need you as a friend."

I smiled and placed my hand on his cheek.

"You're an amazing guy, Craig, and if I totally lived in Los Angeles and was looking for a relationship, I would pursue you until you had no choice but to date me." I grinned.

"You wouldn't have had to pursue. I would have dated you anyway." He winked.

I spent a couple more days with him at his restaurant and he taught me a thing or two about cooking. We talked more about Maddy and I could see that there was a part of him that might be ready to start living again. I had a plan and I prayed I could pull it off.

"I have work to do," I spoke before leaving his restaurant.

"Can you wait a few minutes and I'll send you back with some carry out?"

"I think you've read my mind, Mr. Pines." I grinned as I tapped his chest. "I'll just be at the bar waiting."

About fifteen minutes later, Craig walked over and handed me a plastic bag filled with food.

The Interview: New York & Los Angeles

"Do you have plans tomorrow morning?" I asked.

"Besides being here, no. Why? Do you want to do something?"

"I was thinking we could meet for coffee around ten o'clock at that coffeehouse down the street."

"I'll be there." He smiled. "By the way, when are you heading back to Seattle?"

"I'm not sure yet. Why? Are you sick of me already?"

"No." He laughed. "It's just I'm going to miss you."

"I'll miss you too, but we have these handy little things." I held up my phone. "I'll see you tomorrow morning. Thanks for the food." I kissed his cheek.

I began to walk away and stopped. Setting down the bag, I turned around, walked over to him, and hugged him tight.

"What's that for?"

"I just felt like giving you a hug."

Chapter Twelve

Once I got back to the hotel, I went and sat on the balcony. With my phone in hand, I sent a text message to Maddy asking her to meet me at the coffee shop tomorrow morning. The two of them deserved happiness again and if I could make that happen, then my job here was done. With a prompt reply, she agreed.

I went back inside the room, ate dinner, grabbed my laptop, and started writing the article about Craig. The words came as fast as I could type them, and I smiled at the recollection of events and the time we spent together. As I was in thought, my phone rang, and Eric's face appeared.

"Hey, Eric."

"Your time is up in Los Angeles. No more excuses. I'm not paying for another day there."

"Chill out. I'm hopping on a plane to New York tomorrow. Since it's already Wednesday, I'm going to try and get that interview with Wyatt Coleman, go to the ballet, and with any luck, I'll be back in Seattle on Sunday."

"Oh. So, you do have a plan. I was almost thinking that you weren't ever leaving Los Angeles. I miss you, kid. Hurry up and get back here. George misses you too."

"I will, Eric."

The Interview: New York & Los Angeles

The next morning, I showered, got dressed, and packed my suitcase. Taking one last look around the room, I grabbed my carryon and wheeled my suitcase behind me. It was nine forty-five when I walked through the doors of the coffee house.

"Hi, how can I help you?" the delightful redhead behind the counter asked.

"I need a place to hide out for a few moments. Perhaps behind that door?" I pointed.

"Excuse me?" She shot me a look of confusion.

"I'm on a mission, and in about ten minutes, two people will walk into this coffee house and their destiny will be sealed. I can't let them see me, but I have to know they met before I leave."

"Oh my God." The redhead placed her hand over her heart. "That is so romantic. Come over here." She waved her hand.

"Thank you." I smiled as she opened the door for me.

I looked at my watch. It was nine fifty-five. I stood behind the door, leaving it open a crack so I could see when Craig and Maddy walked in. The bell above the shop door lightly dinged and Maddy walked inside and up to the counter. After ordering a cup of coffee, she took a seat at a small round table with two chairs.

Ten o'clock on the dot and Craig walked into the coffee house. He looked around and his eyes locked on Maddy's.

"Aren't you the owner of Rosie's?" she asked.

I could see the nervousness rise up in him as he tucked his hands into his pants pockets.

"Yes, I am. Craig Pines." He extended his hand.

"Maddy Burkhart. I just love your restaurant. I dine there frequently." She lightly smiled.

"Yes, of course. I've seen you there. You sit at the same table every time you come in. I'm meeting someone here, so I'm going to grab a cup of coffee. Can I get you something?" he asked, and my heart melted.

"Thank you, but I'm all set." Maddy smiled as she held up her cup.

Craig gave her a slight nod and walked up to the counter. Pulling his phone from his pocket, he sent me a text message.

"I'm at the coffee house. Where are you?"

Thank God I had my ringer turned off. He grabbed his coffee from the counter and walked over to Maddy.

"My friend is late," he spoke as he looked at his watch.

"So is mine." She smiled. "Why don't you have a seat while you wait for your friend." Maddy gestured to the empty chair across from her.

"Don't mind if I do. Thank you."

The redhead carefully opened the door and I stood to the side, so they wouldn't see me.

"That's them, isn't it?" she asked with excitement.

"Yes. That's them." I smiled.

"Good job." She patted my shoulder before walking out.

I stood there, staring out as Maddy and Craig talked, smiled, and laughed. Craig was so absorbed in his conversation with her that he didn't check his phone once to see if I had messaged him back. In fact, it seemed the two of them forgot they were supposed to be meeting me. I grabbed my suitcase with a smile and walked out the back door to the alley and came up around the corner from the coffee house. Luckily enough, there was an Uber nearby that picked me up and drove me to the airport.

The Interview: New York & Los Angeles

Bella's *Swan Lake* performance was in three days, which gave me enough time to get that interview with Wyatt Coleman. Before walking up to the ticket counter, I headed over to a quiet spot and phoned Coleman Enterprises.

"Wyatt Coleman's office, Tamara speaking. How may I help you?"

"Hello, Tamara. My name is Laurel Holloway and I would like to speak with Mr. Coleman."

"I'm sorry, Miss Holloway, but Mr. Coleman is out of town."

"Oh. Do you know when he'll be back?"

"He's expected back Sunday night. Is there something I can help you with?"

"I'm with the *Seattle Times* and I would like to interview Mr. Coleman for a magazine article."

"I'm sorry, but Mr. Coleman doesn't do interviews."

I sighed as I rolled my eyes. "Of course, he doesn't. Thank you."

I ended the call and looked up at the ceiling.

"Really?"

I needed to think as I walked around, tapping my phone against my forehead. Suddenly, it rang, and Craig's name appeared on the screen.

"Hey there, big guy," I answered. "Miss me already?"

"You could have at least said goodbye," he spoke.

"And make it harder than it had to be?"

"I know what you did, Laurel."

"How did it go?" I nervously asked.

"We're going on a date tomorrow night."

"Aw, Craig. I'm so happy to hear that."

"Turns out she loves to surf."

"Bonus points." I laughed as tears stung my eyes.

"Yeah. For sure. Where are you headed?"

"New York. To see my sister dance in *Swan Lake*."

"Sounds like fun."

"Not really. My whole dysfunctional family will be there."

"Including the pool boy?" I heard a subtle laugh escape him.

"It wouldn't surprise me."

"When is the ballet?"

"Saturday night. Before then, I have to try and snag one last interview with another single millionaire under the age of thirty-five."

"Uh-oh. That could be dangerous," he spoke.

"I'll be fine."

"I wasn't talking about you. I was referring to him. This guy doesn't know what's coming his way." He laughed. "Thank you, Laurel, for everything. Please keep in touch. I'm really going to miss you."

"You big softie. Stop it." A single tear fell down my cheek. "You keep in touch as well. I want a play by play of your date with Maddy. I'll miss you too. But we do have Facetime, so I'm counting on seeing your handsome face appear on my phone screen."

The Interview: New York & Los Angeles

"Definitely," he spoke. "Have a safe flight to New York."

"Thanks, Craig. I'll talk to you soon."

I ended the call and lowered my phone to my chest with a hint of sadness. I was going to miss him. Just as I was about to phone Eric, his face appeared on my screen.

"I was just going to call you," I answered with a smile.

"Where are you?" he asked as his neck strained to view my surrounding area. "Is that the airport?"

"Yes, and I'm headed to New York. I was hoping to get the interview either today or tomorrow. But, when I called Coleman Enterprises, his secretary said he's out of town until Sunday. Oh, and he doesn't do interviews."

"I know he doesn't, but you'll get one. That's why I sent you."

"I'm just going to spend a few days in New York and see my sister perform. I'll finish the article on Craig Pines and make a plan to get that interview on Monday."

"Sounds like a plan, Laurel, but this is taking a lot longer than I thought. You spent too much time in L.A."

"You got your interview, didn't you?"

"I won't rest until I see it."

"I'll work on it on the plane, Eric. Have to go now. I need to get to my gate. Bye." I hit the end button.

Chapter Thirteen

New York Bound

Walking up to the ticket counter, I purchased my ticket and had enough time to grab a coffee before boarding the plane. As I was standing in line, my eye scanned the man in front of me from head to toe. He was about six feet three inches tall, well-groomed short brownish blond hair, and dressed in a tailored, expensive-as-shit black designer suit. Clean musky and earthy scents infiltrated the space between us. My pheromones were running wild and I desperately needed to see the rest of him. I was betting my life his eyes were dark and mysterious.

It was his turn as he ordered a small regular coffee with a splash of almond milk. I was next.

"What can I get for you?" the barista asked.

"A long black Americano with a double shot of espresso, please."

I handed the barista some cash and stepped to the side, next to sexy man who was now standing with his back still turned, talking on his phone. His coffee was ready, but he didn't hear it being called, so I grabbed it from the counter and tapped him on the shoulder. The moment he turned around, I swallowed hard at the beautiful green eyes that stared back at me.

"This is yours." I smiled.

The Interview: New York & Los Angeles

"Hold on, Charles. Thank you," he spoke while he stared into my eyes as he took the cup from my hand.

My coffee was called, so I grabbed it from the counter, and when I turned back around, he was gone. Shit. Oh well, at least I had a fleeting moment of godly sexiness in front of my eyes. Sighing, I grabbed my carryon and headed to the restroom before boarding the plane. By the time I was finished and arrived at my gate, they had already called first class. Quickly running up, I handed my ticket to the attendant and stepped onto the passenger boarding bridge. Once I reached the plane, I glanced at my ticket for my seat number. I gulped when I turned the corner and saw godly sexiness sitting across from seat 3C, his beautiful green eyes looking at me. Five glorious hours of having the privilege to stare at that fine man made this flight all that much more worth it.

As I sat down, I looked over at my seat buddy, the young woman sitting next to me, and noticed her red swollen eyes. She'd either been crying or had one hell of a hangover. My eyes diverted over to the man across the aisle who was typing away on his phone. The captain came on the overhead and prepared us for takeoff. As the plane took off down the runway, I thought about how I still hadn't told my sister that I was coming in early. I was torn if I wanted to stay at her place or get a hotel room. Her place would be better since I was paying for this part of my New York trip myself.

Chapter Fourteen

Once we were up in the air, I took out my laptop, connected to Wi-Fi, and sent Bella a message.

"Hey baby sister, I'm on a plane to New York as I'm writing this. I needed to fly in a couple days early. Can I crash at your place?"

"Hey, sis. Actually, Mom, Dad, and Alfie just got here a couple of hours ago. Mom and Dad are in the spare bedroom and Alfie is on the couch. So, if you don't mind taking the floor, it's totally cool that you crash here."

What the fuck? Why the hell were my mom, dad, and Alfie already there? Change of plans.

"Hey, it's all cool. I'll get a hotel room or an Airbnb."

"Are you sure? It'll be really good to have you here with us."

"I'm sure. I'll see you soon."

I googled Airbnb in New York City and the first one that popped up looked amazing. The best part, it was only $199 a night for a one-bedroom, two-private-bathroom loft in Manhattan. The pictures looked too good to be true. I clicked on the contact form and asked if it was still available. I nervously waited for a response as I scrolled through the pictures.

The Interview: New York & Los Angeles

"Apartment hunting?" The godly sexy man smirked.

For the love of God, my stomach started to flutter as my legs tightened.

"Airbnb," I responded.

"I take it you're not from New York?"

"No. Seattle. I'm flying in to see my sister dance in *Swan Lake*."

"Interesting." The corners of his mouth slightly curved upwards. "And you didn't think to book something sooner?"

"Actually, I didn't. I was just in Los Angeles for business and I wasn't a hundred percent sure I was leaving until this morning."

Why the hell was I telling a complete stranger all this? That's right. He was sexy as fuck and I wanted to keep the conversation with him going for as long as I could.

Suddenly, a reply came back from the owner of the Airbnb, Carol.

"Hi Laurel. You're in luck. We did have it rented out for the next few days, but the renter had to cancel. If you're interested, it's yours. How many nights did you need it for?"

"Excellent. I'll need it for four nights and I'll be checking out Sunday morning."

"All I'll need is your credit card information and it's yours."

I pulled my card from my wallet and typed in the number.

"Great. I'll text you the address and my phone number. Just give me a call when you get into the city and I'll meet you at the apartment."

"Thank you, Carol."

"Yes!" I exclaimed. Maybe a little too loudly.

"Good news?" the sexy godly man asked.

"The Airbnb I inquired about is available." I smiled.

"Pity. I was hoping you wouldn't find a place and you could stay with me." He winked.

Holy shit, I think I just orgasmed.

"Then you should have said something sooner." I arched my brow.

His mouth flowed into a full smile as he let out a chuckle. "Damn. I'm always a little too late. If you'll excuse me, I have some work to do."

"Me too." I smirked.

Damn. This guy was totally turning me on. I needed to focus on finishing up my article about Craig. As I was writing and doing some editing, I heard subtle sniffles coming from my seat buddy. When I glanced over at her, she was quietly crying while looking out the window of the plane. *Damn it.*

"Are you okay?" I asked as I lightly placed my hand on her arm.

"No. I'm not." She wiped her eyes.

"Would you like to talk about it? I'm a really good listener."

"No. I can't." She cried harder.

"Okay." I turned back to my laptop.

The last thing I needed while trying to work was this chick crying her eyes out next to me. It was bad enough I was distracted by the man across the aisle, who was working but would steal small glances here and there.

"I saw my boyfriend with another girl," my seat buddy

blurted out. "He just moved to L.A. for his job and in a few months when I was finished with school, I was going to move out there with him. I wanted to surprise him with a visit, so I didn't tell him I was coming."

"Let me guess, you found them in bed together?"

"No, but I saw them outside his apartment kissing when the cab driver pulled up. I was so sick to my stomach that I told the cab driver to take me back to the airport. I don't know what to do," she sobbed.

"Did you text him or call him after you saw them?"

"No. I can't. I hate him right now and I might say something I will regret."

"Listen, sweetie. The fact is that he's seeing another woman. There's nothing you can say right now that you'll regret. How long have the two of you been dating?"

"Six months."

"Six months isn't a long time. He did you a favor. It's better that you found out now instead of next year, or worse yet, when you moved there to be with him. Guys are assholes," I voiced a little too loudly.

The sexy godly man across the aisle loudly cleared his throat. When I looked over at him, he looked at me with an arch in his brow. I shrugged and continued talking with my seat buddy.

"Were you ever cheated on?" she asked.

"As a matter of fact, I was, and it hurts. I know what you're feeling and going through. I promise you it will get better. If you want my advice, send him a break up text. Don't give him the satisfaction of you knowing that he's cheating. You have the power now, and the only person who can make you feel better is you. And whatever you do, don't give him an explanation of why you're breaking up. If you want to really get him, tell him you met someone else. He doesn't deserve you. You're a young beautiful girl, and there are so many men out there that would be honored to call you their girlfriend. Don't waste your energy on some douchebag who has to put his dick into every vagina he meets just to make himself feel less insecure."

"It hurts so much." She sniffled.

"I know it does." I gave her hand a gentle squeeze. "But there's a lesson behind every broken heart. Each pain is a new opportunity to love yourself even more. Don't ever depend on someone else to give you what you can give yourself, and that's respect."

"You're right. He was a loser anyway. I can do so much better than him."

"That's right, sister! He doesn't deserve you."

"Thank you—"

"Laurel," I softly spoke.

"I'm Renee. I'm sorry for spilling all my problems like that."

"Please." I smiled. "I was the one who asked, and I was more than happy to listen. Sometimes, it's easier to talk to a stranger."

"Yeah. You're right. I'll let you get back to work. I think I'm going to take a nap."

The Interview: New York & Los Angeles

Chapter Fifteen

Concentrating on my article was hard with sexy godly man sitting across from me. Shit, what I wouldn't give to see what kind of package he was sporting under that sexy designer suit. There was definitely some sexual chemistry between us. I could see the hunger in his eyes when he looked at me. Believe me, I was no stranger when it came to that look.

The plane landed, and I was finally in New York. I gave Renee a hug and told her to stay strong.

"After you." The sexy godly man smiled as he gestured me to exit my seat first.

"Thank you." I seductively grinned.

I felt the placement of his hand on my lower back and I began to tremble. As soon as we exited the plane, he lightly grabbed my arm.

"This way," he spoke as he led me to the left.

"I'm sorry, but what are you doing and where are we going?"

"There's no denying that we both want to fuck each other. So, we need to do it and get it out of our systems."

"Excuse me?" I turned to him as I silently smiled. "I don't even know your name."

"Names don't matter when two people are physically

attracted to each other," he spoke as he opened the door to a family restroom, then locked it once we were inside. "Plus, we'll never see each other again."

He placed his hands on my face while his mouth meshed with mine for a moment.

"Take your dress off," he demanded. "I want to see if my imagination is on point." He smirked.

"Well, I have an imagination too, so you first." I gestured with my hand.

"That's not how it works, sweetheart."

I stood there, my head cocked to the side as the pulsating vibration down below was screaming at me to just do what he said.

"Fine, then we'll do it at the same time. I'm not going to stand here naked while you stand there fully clothed gawking at me." My brow raised.

His eye narrowed as he studied me for a moment.

"I do have morals," I spoke.

He let out a chuckle. "If you had morals, you wouldn't be in an airport about to have sex with a perfect stranger."

"Same goes for you," I spoke.

"I never said I had any morals."

Shit. He just made himself a whole lot sexier.

"Dress off," he commanded.

"Pants off," I commanded back. "Judging by the bulge down there, I'm thinking you need to release it ASAP."

He took in an irritated breath. "Who the hell are you?"

The Interview: New York & Los Angeles

I shrugged. "Apparently a woman you want to fuck." I smirked.

"Damn it," he growled as he fumbled with his belt, stepped out of his pants, and hung them on the hook that was attached to the door.

I reached behind me and unzipped the short black sundress I was wearing, letting it fall to the ground. Maybe not such a good choice since we were in a public restroom. His eyes raked over me in my black lace strapless pushup bra and matching black lace panties, as mine did over him in his black boxer briefs with a bulge that made me swallow hard.

"You are one hell of a sexy woman," he muttered as he took a couple steps towards me.

"And you are one hell of a sexy man," I replied.

His fingers went straight to the sides of my panties as his lips met with mine. My body tingled from head to toe as our tongues met and his finger dipped inside me. Taking his free hand, he reached behind me and unhooked my bra with one swift movement. His fingers went right for my hard nipples as he played with them.

"You're getting wetter by the second," he muttered in between kisses. "I love how excited your body is."

His mouth left mine and his tongue trailed across my collarbone and down to my breasts that were so freely staring him in the face. His mouth gently wrapped around my hardened peak as he lightly bit it and then soothed it with the softness of his tongue. My body was in freaking overdrive and I wanted him like an animal in heat. He was teasing me, and as much as I appreciated it at first, I was ready to get down and dirty. His finger explored me, hitting the spot that sent me into a rapid orgasmic state. His arm held me as I threw my head back and let out subtle sounds of pleasure and my legs tightened around his masculine hand.

"That was just the appetizer." He smiled.

As I tried to catch my breath, I quickly took down his underwear and stared at his neatly trimmed package and large sex toy that stood full attention.

"Does it meet your expectations?" he asked in a low voice as he held his cock in his hand.

"Oh yes." My heart rapidly pounded.

I got down on my knees, the cement floor digging into them, as I curled my lips around my teeth and slowly placed my mouth around his tip. A groan erupted in his chest as I dipped my head and took him in all the way. My fingers swept across his balls as my head moved up and down. I didn't think he could get any harder than he already was, but he did. Several moans escaped him as he grabbed my hair and held it in his hands.

"Enough," he commanded. "I don't want to come yet."

I stood up and licked my lips as he reached inside his pants pocket and took out a condom. Ripping open the foil as quickly as he could, he rolled the latex over his cock, picked me up, and set me on the long counter next to the sink. He pulled me to the edge as his mouth devoured my pussy, making sure I was wet enough to take him inside me.

"Are you ready for the entrée?" he asked. "I'm not going to lie, it might hurt a little."

"Give me all you got." I arched my brow with a smile.

The corners of his mouth curved upwards as he placed his hands on my hips and thrust inside me. His lips met mine as I welcomed him, and he pushed himself inch by inch until he was buried deep within me. My nails clawed his back as he rapidly fucked me like a beast. In and out, fast, but with smooth strokes. My skin heated like a blaze of fire and my heart rapidly beat as my breath became shallow. Beads of sweat formed on his forehead as his mouth smashed into mine. Our lips tangled, and

The Interview: New York & Los Angeles

our tongues twisted as we both let out carnal sounds of pleasure.

"Is this what you wanted?" he asked. "Is this what you needed?"

"Yes," I breathlessly spoke as I threw my head back and his tongue stroked my neck.

"Goddamn it, you feel so good," he whispered.

My legs tightened around him as my body sank into another mind-blowing orgasm. He wasn't far behind as his thrusts became slower for two more pumps and then he halted inside me, moaning as he came while his hands tightened their grip on my hips. He looked at me before resting his forehead against mine, both of us out of breath. I had no words for what I just experienced. For the first time in my life, I was speechless.

He pulled out, tossed the condom in the trash, and began to get dressed.

"Here." He winked as he handed me my panties, bra, and dress.

"Thank you."

"Have fun in New York," he spoke as he buttoned up his shirt.

"So far, I am." I smiled.

"It was nice to meet you—"

"Names don't matter, remember? And I'm sure you meant it was nice to fuck me."

"Right. That too." He grinned.

He walked over to the door and placed his hand on the knob, hesitating for about twenty seconds before turning it and walking out. Once the door shut, I turned around and placed my hands on the sink while staring at myself in the mirror.

"It was only sex, Laurel," I spoke to myself. "It doesn't matter if he was the best thing since apple pie. He was nothing more than a one-day stand, and you'll never see him again."

I took in a deep breath, grabbed my purse and my carryon, and walked out of the bathroom.

The Interview: New York & Los Angeles

Chapter Sixteen

When I climbed into the cab that was parked at the curb outside the airport, I gave the driver the address to the Airbnb. I couldn't stop thinking about sexy godly man and how disoriented he left me. I needed to talk to George, so I dialed his number and prayed he answered.

"Hey, Laurel. I'm in a meeting with Eric. Can I call you back?"

"No. I need to talk to you now. It's important."

"We're in a meeting, Laurel," Eric's voice spoke.

Shit. George must have had me on speaker.

"Take me off speaker, George," I spoke.

"Whatever you have to say to George, you can say to me. Make it quick, though."

Rolling my eyes, I sighed. Oh well, it was only Eric.

"Fine. I just had sex with this amazing guy in the airport."

"Whoa!" Eric exclaimed. "Go, George. We can continue this later."

"What do you mean?" George spoke in a low voice.

"I met this guy, well, I didn't get his name, but he was on my flight. He sat in the aisle seat across from me. George, the physical attraction was unreal. And the sex, holy shit, I can't even describe it."

"Why didn't you get his name?" he asked.

"He said names weren't important. This guy, this man, he was—"

"Laurel, this doesn't sound like you."

"I know and it's freaking me the fuck out. What do I do?"

"You didn't get his name, so there's nothing you can do. It's not like you can find him again in a city with millions of people. Just try to forget about it and remember why you're in New York."

"That's the problem. I don't want to remember why I'm in New York. He was a distraction, and I just found out on the plane my whole family is here already."

He let out a long sigh. "Laurel, sweetheart, you know I love you, but I don't know what to tell you. You're just going to have to try and forget about him. It was only sex, just the way you like it."

"I know. Bummer."

"Well, look at it this way, you're on cloud nine right now, so dealing with your family should be a breeze."

"I'm not so sure about that, George. Anyway, I just arrived at my Airbnb. I'll talk to you later."

"Bye, love. Try not to stress. You're in New York. Have the time of your life. It's already starting off on a good foot."

I ended the call, grabbed my suitcase, and went up to Apartment 6B. When I arrived, the door was slightly opened.

"Hello." I lightly knocked as I walked inside.

The Interview: New York & Los Angeles

"You must be Laurel." A tall woman with long blonde hair greeted me.

"And you must be Carol. It's nice to meet you."

"Nice to meet you too. Let me show you around."

The apartment looked even better than the pictures online and I knew I made the right choice by staying here instead of a hotel. Plus, this place had a washer and dryer and I needed to do some laundry. After I put the last load in the dryer, my phone rang, and it was Bella.

"Hello," I answered.

"Hey. Are you in New York yet?"

"Umm. Yeah. I just stepped off the plane." I lied.

"Great. I've made reservations for all of us at seven o'clock at Patsy's. Mom is craving Italian. We'll see you there. I'll text you the address."

Great. Dinner with the Holloway clan. I could hardly wait.

"Okay. I'll see you at seven," I spoke.

"Which hotel are you staying at?" she asked. "We can come pick you up."

"I'm staying at an Airbnb. I'll just meet you there."

"Oh. Okay. I'm super excited to see you. It seems like it's been forever."

"Me too. I'll see you guys at seven."

I ended the call and took a seat on the couch, bringing my knees up to my chest and thinking about sexy godly man. I hated this. This was not what I did. This was not me. I laid down for a while and took a nap, hoping that when I woke up, he would be nothing but a distant memory. It didn't work, so I got up, showered, and began getting ready for dinner with the Holloways.

I was fashionably late by ten minutes when I walked into Patsy's and told the hostess that I was meeting my family. I took in a deep breath while she led me over to a large round table where they sat.

"Laurel, sweetheart." My dad smiled as he stood up and kissed my cheek.

"Hey, Dad."

I walked around and kissed the cheeks of my brother and sister, and last but not least, my mother.

"It's good to see you, Laurel. It's been quite a while," she spoke.

"I know. I've been crazy busy with work."

"Who's the new man in your life?" she asked as she picked up her drink.

"I'm not seeing anyone right now," I replied.

"You're twenty-seven years old, Laurel. Don't you think it's time you thought about settling down?" my father asked. "Look at Alfie here." He hooked his arm around him. "He's going to propose to Celia on her birthday, and Bella has been dating Thaddeus for a year now."

"And give up my many one-night stands?" I grinned. "Never."

My father didn't say a word and my mother cleared her throat before kicking back her tequila.

"I don't know why you aren't staying with us at Bella's apartment," she spoke.

"Because I'm not sleeping on the floor. By the way, what are

The Interview: New York & Los Angeles

you all doing here so early? I figured you wouldn't be flying in until Friday night."

"Your father has a meeting here tomorrow, so we thought we'd fly in early and take in New York."

Lucky me. I should have stayed in L.A. for a couple more days. I heard my phone chime, and when I pulled it from my purse, I noticed a text message from Alfie.

"Hey, is it okay if I stay with you at your Airbnb for a couple of days?"

I looked up as his brow arched in a begging sort of way.

"Sure."

"Thanks. I owe you."

"Alfie, Laurel, put your phones away," my mother spoke. "You know I don't like phones out during dinner."

I rolled my eyes and set my phone back in my purse. As I sat there and listened to them talk amongst themselves, my mind kept diverting back to sexy godly man.

"Laurel, Bella has rehearsal all day tomorrow, Alfie is meeting some friends, and your father will be in meetings, so how about we do some shopping on Fifth Avenue?" my mother asked.

The way she put it was as if I was her last choice because she would have nothing else to do. Against my better judgment, I told her yes. Once dinner was over, Bella asked me to come back to her apartment to hang out for a while.

"As much as I'd love to, I'm exhausted. It's been a long day," I spoke.

"Oh, okay. Well, tonight is the only night I had free."

I could sense the disappointment in her voice and a part of

me felt bad.

"I'm going to be here for a few more days anyway on business. We can catch up then?"

"Okay." She smiled.

Once we were outside and I was saying goodbye to my parents, Alfie lightly took hold of my arm and whispered in my ear.

"I'm going to grab my stuff at Bella's and then head to your place. Text me the address."

"Sure thing," I spoke.

I climbed into a cab and took it back to the apartment. About an hour later, Alfie was at my door.

"Hey, thanks for letting me stay here."

"No problem. What did Mom and Dad say?"

"They were cool with it. I'm heading out to meet a friend of mine. Don't wait up."

I laughed. "Have I ever waited up?"

"No." He smiled as he kissed my cheek. "We'll catch up in the morning, okay?"

"Okay. Have fun. Don't do anything I wouldn't do." I pointed at him.

After I took a long hot bath and climbed into bed, it was midnight. I was tired, and as much as I tried to sleep, I couldn't get him or the sex out of my mind and it drove me insane.

The Interview: New York & Los Angeles

Chapter Seventeen

The next morning, I was woken up by the ringing sound of my phone. Reaching over and grabbing it from the nightstand, I saw Eric was facetiming me.

"Hello," I sleepily answered.

"Did I wake you?" he asked as he sat behind his desk.

"What do you think?"

"Well, you need to be up anyway. Where's my article on Craig Pines?"

"I was going to send it as soon as I got up."

"Good, you're up, so send it now."

"For fuck sakes, Eric. Can I get a cup of coffee first?"

"Fine. Get your coffee and send my article."

I looked over at the clock and noticed it was nine fifteen.

"Why are you in the office so early? Isn't it six fifteen there?"

"It sure is. The early bird always catches the worm." He grinned.

"You're a real go getter, Eric. Give me a few minutes and you'll have your article. Now don't bug me anymore until

Sunday. I'm officially off work time."

"I know. I know." He put his hand up. "Enjoy New York."

"Thanks."

I ended the call, climbed out of bed, and walked towards the kitchen. I gasped when I passed the pullout couch and saw Alfie lying there with some girl wrapped in his arms. Shaking my head, I popped a k-cup in the Keurig and waited for my coffee to brew. I also made it known that I was in the kitchen by being exceptionally loud.

"Oh hey. I'm Ari." The perky brunette smiled. "You must be Alfie's sister."

"I am." I stared her down.

"Hey, sis." Alfie yawned as he strolled into the kitchen.

"Really, little brother?"

I picked up my coffee cup and took it over to the table where my laptop was sitting. Opening it up, I glanced over the article one last time and hit the send button. One down, one to go.

"I have to get going. It was nice meeting you," Ari spoke.

"You too." I nodded.

Alfie kissed her goodbye and took a seat at the table next to me.

"What are you doing, Alfie? You're proposing to Celia."

"So? I'm not married yet." He smiled.

"You're a pig," I spat. "And you have no respect for women."

"That's not true. I love Celia. I think."

"What do you mean you 'think'?"

The Interview: New York & Los Angeles

"I don't know, sis." He sighed. "I just feel like it's what I'm supposed to do. Settle down, start a family."

"Why? Because that's what Dad wants you to do?"

"Maybe." He shrugged.

"If you truly loved Celia, you wouldn't be banging Ari. Don't do something because it's what's expected of you. Be your own person, Alfie. Live life on your terms. Not Mom and Dad's."

"You mean like you?" His brow arched.

"Yes, exactly like me."

"But the difference is you left. I can't, and I'm constantly under their thumb. Plus, Mom and Dad love Celia. They said she's perfect for me."

"Is she perfect for you? Do you believe she is?" I asked as I placed my hand on his.

"I don't know. She has social status. She comes from a good family and she loves me."

"You don't marry someone for their social status. Look at our parents. Is that really the kind of life you want to live?"

"If I can have my cake and eat it too, sure."

"Ugh. You're impossible. I have to go get ready to meet Mom."

"Good luck with that." He laughed.

"Thanks." I brushed my hand over his head.

****

Shopping with my mother was an adventure. Let me tell you. I'd heard it all.

"Laurel, why can't you find a good man? Laurel, why don't you get your hair cut in a shorter style? It'll make you look more professional. Laurel, I'm noticing some lines in your forehead. Have you considered Botox? Men like a flawless face. Laurel, have you considered getting your breasts enhanced?"

OH MY GOD I was ready to rip my hair out. Everything about me with her was negative. I had yet to hear her say one positive thing. After we ate a late lunch, I was more than ready to get back to my Airbnb.

"I'm going to head back to the apartment. I have to do some work for Everything Laurel."

"Are you going to continue doing that column for the rest of your life?" she asked.

I stopped and cocked my head at her.

"What's wrong with my column?" I asked.

"Nothing. I just thought you'd want to do bigger things."

I took in a deep breath and refused to engage, because if I did, that would be the end of our relationship, mother or not.

"I like what I do," I simply spoke. "I'll see you guys Saturday night."

"What are you going to be doing the next couple of days that you can't spend time with us?" she asked.

"I'm going to try and get that interview, so I can get back to Seattle."

"I see. Well, your father, Alfie, and I are having dinner at the Plaza Hotel before the performance. Can you at least join us?"

"I don't know, Mom." I sighed. "I'll have to let you know."

"Whatever, Laurel. I'll let your father know," she spoke as she climbed into a cab.

The Interview: New York & Los Angeles

"Go ahead and let him know. I don't really care," I mumbled to myself.

****

I spent the next two days going to museums, spending some time in Central Park, and pampering myself with a mani/pedi and a massage. My time spent alone was well worth it. As I was sitting on the couch with a cup of coffee in my hands and looking out the window, there was a knock on the door. Getting up, I was surprised when I answered it and my dad was standing there.

"Hello, sweetheart." He smiled as he kissed my forehead.

"Dad, what are you doing here?"

"I think we need to have a little talk. May I come in?"

"Of course."

He stepped inside and took a look around.

"Not bad." He nodded his head. "But you could have stayed at the Plaza or the Waldorf. I would have paid for your suite."

"I can afford to pay for my own suite, Dad. I was just in a hotel for a few days in California and I wanted something that felt a little more like home."

"I can understand that. Your mother said that you might not be joining us for dinner. Is that true?"

I looked at him as I brought my mug up to my lips.

"I think I'll just meet you guys at the ballet."

"Laurel." He paced around the room. "We barely see you. In fact, I haven't seen you since Wednesday night. The least you can do is have dinner with your family."

I wasn't in the mood to stand there and listen to his lectures.

All I'd have to do was get through dinner and the ballet and then I was family free for a long time.

"You're right, Dad. I'll be there."

"That's my girl." He smiled as he kissed my forehead.

*****

I got through dinner. My mother was too focused on Bella and how excited she was to see her baby girl perform. It was all she talked about. She also went on to sing the praises of Bella's boyfriend, Thaddeus, Mr. Wall Street hotshot. A man who couldn't be bothered to meet us for dinner before the ballet because he was stuck in some meeting. I'd bet my life on it he was stuck in something and it certainly wasn't a meeting. The guy was a huge flirt and I didn't like him. He seemed like a shady motherfucker to me.

We arrived at the Metropolitan Opera House and stood in the lobby while my parents mingled with some friends that they saw. Sipping on my wine and chatting with Alfie, I scanned the crowd.

"Sis, are you okay?" Alfie asked as he handed me a napkin.

"I'm fine," I replied as I wiped the wine that spattered out of my mouth.

He was here. Sexy godly man. The man from the plane. The man I fucked. The man I couldn't stop thinking about since Wednesday. He was standing next to a beautiful woman. Long brown hair, high cheekbones, perfectly shaped almond eyes and a body that any woman would kill for. My heart sank down into my belly. He had a girlfriend or worse, a wife! *Shit.* Fucking douchebag. If there's one thing I didn't do, it was have sex with another woman's man. *DAMN IT!* I balled my fist.

"Something is clearly going on with you, Laurel," Alfie spoke. "Who are you staring at? You look like you're ready to fight."

The Interview: New York & Los Angeles

"See that man over there? The hot and sexy one in the black tux? Brownish-blond hair?"

"Yeah." He stared at him.

"He and I had a thing at the airport when we got off the plane. I didn't know he had a girlfriend," I spoke through gritted teeth.

"I'm sure half the guys you have sex with have girlfriends. You just don't know it." He smirked as he brought his glass up to his lips.

I smacked his chest and glared at him.

"Don't take it out on me. Wait till the girlfriend isn't around and go give him a piece of your mind."

"Oh, I will." I stood there and nodded my head.

"I know you will." Alfie grinned. "And I hope I'm around to see it."

I specifically told him I was flying into New York to see my sister perform in *Swan Lake*. He didn't mention that he was also seeing it. Probably because he didn't want me asking questions about whom he was seeing it with.

The four of us took our seats, and after a few moments, Thaddeus showed up and took the empty seat next to mine. Great. After sucking up to my parents, he sat down and grabbed my hand.

"You look amazing, Laurel. It's good to see you again."

I pulled my hand away and gave him a fake smile. It was shortly before intermission and I desperately needed to use the bathroom, so I told Alfie that I'd meet them out in the lobby. When I was finished, I headed to the lobby and saw godly sexy lying cheating bastard standing alone with a drink in his hand. This was my perfect opportunity to let him know what I thought about him.

"Hey," I harshly spoke as I walked up to him.

"Hello there." He smiled. "I honestly didn't think I'd see you again."

"I'm happy I ran into you because I'm going to tell you exactly what I think of you." I cocked my head.

"Okay?" His brow arched.

"You're nothing but a cheating bastard and I take back having sex with you. It never happened."

He chuckled. "You can't take back sex. It did indeed happen." He grinned. "Anyway, what's this all about?"

"Oh, you know what this is about, asshole! I despise men like you. And you know what?" I pointed my finger at him. "Karma will bite you in the ass one day. One day you'll actually love someone, and they'll hurt you and it'll break your heart. And when that day comes, I hope you'll think of me and this conversation." I turned on my Gucci heels and stomped away. God, it felt good to tell him off.

After the performance, I went back to my Airbnb. As soon as I stepped inside, my phone rang, and Craig's face appeared on the screen.

"Hey there, handsome." I smiled as I answered.

"Hi, beautiful. How's New York treating you?"

"Eh."

"That bad?"

"Let's just say I'm over it. Enough about me and New York. Tell me how your date went."

A big smile crossed his lips.

"It went great. In fact, we're seeing each other again

The Interview: New York & Los Angeles

tomorrow night. I'm cooking dinner for her."

"Wow. I'm not going to lie and say that I'm not jealous. To eat one of your meals again would be heaven."

He chuckled. "You can come back here to L.A. and I'll cook for you anytime you want."

"Trust me. I'll be back." I smiled. "Maddy's pretty great, isn't she?"

"She is. We talked until two a.m. and then I drove her home. We had a good night, Laurel. Thanks again for being such a pain in the ass." He smiled.

"You're welcome, Mr. Pines. Being a pain in the ass is my specialty."

Chapter Eighteen

Sunday had come and gone. I had breakfast with my parents and Alfie before they hopped on a plane back to Boston. Bella said her goodbyes at the apartment because she was too exhausted to join us.

"Don't be a stranger, Laurel." My mother kissed my cheek. "And next time I see you, I hope to see a dashing and handsome young man on your arm."

"I'll try my best, Mom. I think I'll quit my job and scour the world to make that happen for you." I gave a cocky smile.

"Don't be sassy. That's probably the main reason why you're still single."

I clenched my teeth behind my closed smile.

"Like your mother said, don't be a stranger. I hate that we barely get to see you. You need to come home for a visit," my dad spoke as he hugged me. "It's been far too long."

"I know, Dad."

"Bye, sis. Thanks again for letting me crash at your Airbnb," Alfie spoke.

"You're welcome. Have a safe flight home and remember what we talked about." I arched my brow.

They climbed into the limo my father arranged, and when it

The Interview: New York & Los Angeles

pulled away from the curb, I let out a deep breath. I glanced at my watch and noticed I had about an hour before I had to check out of the Airbnb. *Shit*. Now to decide which hotel I was going to stay in. In case you couldn't tell, I'm more of a wing-it type of girl. I was never good at planning because every time I planned something, it would fall through or didn't work out how I wanted it to. By winging everything, there was no disappointment in the end.

I headed back to the Airbnb, took a seat on the couch with my laptop, and began looking up reasonably priced hotels so Eric wouldn't be too upset with me. But reasonably priced and nice in New York City wasn't a duo. I typed the address to Coleman Enterprises in the google search bar. It was best to get a hotel near his office, preferably within walking distance to save on cab fare. I knew Eric would appreciate it. The Surrey came up as being one of the closest. It wasn't cheap but so chic. I grabbed my phone and booked a room. As much as I wanted to stay in one of their suites, Eric would have a heart attack and I didn't feel like hearing it. But, I was lucky enough to get a city view deluxe room. I grabbed my suitcase and my bag, checked out of my Airbnb, and took a cab to The Surrey. All I wanted was to get this damn interview with Wyatt Coleman over with and get the hell out of New York. I was still salty about Mr. Cheating Douchebag, aka sexy godly man.

I decided to utilize the spa at the hotel and had arranged for a massage and facial, which took up a good four hours. When I got back to my room, my phone rang, and Eric's face appeared on the screen. Damn him.

"Hello, Eric," I answered.

"Where are you?"

"New York. Where are you?"

"Very funny, Laurel," he spoke as he tried to check out my room. "That room looks expensive. Which hotel are you at?"

"The Surrey."

"How do you spell that?" he asked as he began typing away on his keyboard.

I spelled it out for him one letter at a time while rolling my eyes.

"Jesus Christ, Laurel. What the hell did I tell you?"

"Calm down. It's only a block from Coleman Enterprises. I can walk. Any cabs I utilize here in the city, I'll pay for myself."

"You better get that interview tomorrow and get the hell back to Seattle." He pointed his finger at the screen. "Have you figured out how you're going to do it yet?"

"I did," I lied.

"Tell me then."

"No, Eric. I don't want to jinx it. And why would you send me here knowing he doesn't do interviews?"

"Because I know you can get one. You're stubborn, ruthless, and don't take no for an answer."

"Thanks. I think." I furrowed my brows.

"Just do it and get home. And by the way, the article better be juicer than Craig Pines."

"You're really putting the pressure on me and it's giving me anxiety."

"Please, Laurel." He rolled his eyes. "You're the toughest woman I've ever known. You thrive under pressure."

"Whatever, Eric. I have to go. I need to work on Everything Laurel so I don't have to worry about it while I'm focusing on Mr. Coleman."

"Have a good night and keep me posted."

"I will, and just so we're clear, I'll call you. Stop calling me!"

"You seem to forget who the boss is in this relationship." His eye narrowed at me.

"Goodbye, Eric." I ended the call.

I ordered room service, stared out at the city view, and then worked diligently on Everything Laurel. I thought long and hard about my plan of action for tomorrow and came up with an idea. Just as I was about to go to sleep, my phone rang, and George's face appeared.

"Hey there." I smiled as I answered his call.

"Are you in bed already?"

"It's eleven o'clock here."

"Shit. That's right. I forgot about the time difference. How's it going?"

"I ran into the guy from the plane last night at the ballet."

"Seriously? Did you talk to him?"

"I did. He was with a woman. I told him exactly what I thought of him."

"Shit, Laurel. What did he say?"

"Nothing. I didn't give him a chance to say anything. I said what I had to and walked away."

"Damn. I wish I could have been there. I love seeing you in fierce action like that." He laughed.

"He's an asshole and I can't wait to get out of this city and come home."

"Aw, I'm sorry. I miss you. When do you think you'll be back?"

"Hopefully, I can hop on a plane Tuesday. I will get that interview with Mr. Coleman tomorrow."

"That's my girl. Go get him, make him talk, and get your ass back here. I miss having you at the office."

"I miss you too." I yawned.

"Get some rest. Call me tomorrow and let me know how it goes."

"I will. Love you."

"Love you too."

The Interview: New York & Los Angeles

Chapter Nineteen

The next morning, I dressed in my sexiest dress, threw some curls at the ends of my hair, and put on my makeup as if I was going out for the evening. Putting on some sunglasses and throwing my stiletto heels in a bag, I walked to Coleman Enterprises. Before I reached the double glass doors, I changed from my flats to my heels. Once I was inside, I looked on the directory for Coleman Enterprises.

"Which floor?" a handsome older gentleman asked as he smiled at me.

"Twentieth, please."

I stood there, calm and confident as the elevator doors opened to the twentieth floor on which I was greeted by a young female with overly dramatic black hair.

"May I help you?"

"I'm looking for Mr. Coleman's office."

"I'm sorry, but Mr. Coleman isn't available."

"I didn't expect he was." I smiled. "I actually need to speak with his secretary, not him."

"Oh. Take this hallway down to the end and make a left. You'll see Tamara sitting at her desk."

"Thank you."

As soon as I made a left at the end of the hallway, I found his secretary, approximately early forties, blonde hair secured in a tight bun, and red lips that were blinding, sitting behind her desk typing away at her computer.

"Excuse me," I spoke in a soft voice.

"Yes." She looked up at me.

"I need to speak with Mr. Coleman. Is he in there?" I pointed to his office.

"Mr. Coleman is unavailable. May I ask who you are?"

"That's not important." I waved my hand. "What's important is that I need to speak with him right away."

"I'm sorry, but that won't be possible."

"Anything's possible." I graciously smiled. "Listen, Tamara. You seem like a nice woman, and very stylish, may I add. I know you're doing your job and you're doing it very well, but see, I have a problem. I need to speak to Mr. Coleman about a personal matter, an encounter that happened a couple of nights ago without my consent. Now, you can let me see him so the two of us can discuss it like mature adults, or I can call the police and totally make it public. Your call." I smiled.

Nervously, she cleared her throat and got up from her seat.

"May I tell him your name?"

"He didn't get my name when the encounter happened."

Her eyes looked frightened and I felt bad, but I had no other choice. Once I got to talk to him, I would clear things up with Tamara.

"What the hell is going—" He stopped dead in the doorway.

"Oh hell no! No. No. No."

The Interview: New York & Los Angeles

The corners of his mouth curved up into a strong smile as he stared at me.

"Come into my office. You have some explaining to do," he spoke. "Tamara, it's okay. You may go back to your desk."

"Of course, Mr. Coleman."

Fuck my life. Sexy godly man was none other than Wyatt Coleman.

"Have a seat." He gestured.

"I'll stand. Thank you." I cocked my head at him as my heart pounded out of my chest.

"I asked you to sit down." His voice was commanding.

"And I told you that I prefer to stand." I crossed my arms.

"Fine." He threw his hands up in the air. "Now that you're here, would you like to tell me why you're stalking me?"

A rip-roaring laugh escaped me. *Was he serious? Stalking him?*

"You think I'm—" I pointed to myself. "I'm—stalking you?" I laughed.

"Yes. And why is that so damn funny? First of all, you show up at the ballet on Saturday night and tell me off like some kind of psychopath and now you're lying to my secretary to get my attention. I know why you're doing this." He pointed his finger at me. "It's because we had sex at the airport."

My jaw dropped as I stood there and listened to him spew his bullshit.

"First of all, who the hell do you think you are? I specifically told you on the airplane that I was attending the ballet to see my sister perform. How the hell did I know you were going to be there? Did you say that you'd be there as well? No. You didn't.

And second of all, sex with you wasn't all that, mister." I totally lied through my teeth. "Certainly not worth stalking you over. Gee, you are so stuck on yourself." I placed my hands on my hips.

"Then why did you feel the need to tell me off Saturday night?" His head cocked to the side.

"Because you have a girlfriend and you're out having sex with other women behind her back. That's why. You're a total douchebag!"

"I don't have a girlfriend. The woman you saw me with was my sister, Sammi. The ballet was an early birthday present for her."

"Oh." I slithered into the chair across from his desk. "I didn't know."

"How would you? You didn't even give me a chance to explain that night. You flew off in a tizzy like the psycho woman you are."

I sat there with a narrowed eye, feeling like a complete idiot.

"I apologize for that. And for the record, I'm not a psycho. I just don't like men who cheat."

"Whether or not you're a psycho has yet to be determined. You never answered my other question. Why are you here in my office? How the hell did you even find me?" He leaned back in his black executive chair.

"My name is Laurel Holloway and I work for the *Seattle Times*. We're creating a magazine called *Daily Fusion* and I was sent to interview you for it. Self-made millionaires under the age of thirty-five. But I didn't know that was you fucking me in the bathroom at the airport."

"You just randomly show up for interviews without even calling or scheduling one?"

The Interview: New York & Los Angeles

"I called, and your secretary told me you don't do interviews."

"I don't." His brow raised. "So, if you already knew that I didn't do them, why are you here?"

"Because it's my job, Mr. Coleman. And by the way, little Miss Tamara out there specifically told me that you were out of town until last night, yet you were on my plane right after I called."

"I came back early and forgot to mention it to her. So as far as she was concerned, I wasn't coming back until last night."

"Then how did you get the tickets for the ballet for your sister if you weren't supposed to be back until last night?"

The corners of his mouth curved upwards. "You're quite inquisitive."

"I'm a journalist. It's my job."

"I purchased them when I came back. Her birthday isn't until Wednesday. But, since I got back from my trip early, I wanted to take her. She's been talking about it for months."

"My sister told me the tickets had been sold out for weeks."

"I have connections, Miss Holloway."

"Of course you do." I smirked. "I should've known. All rich men like you have connections."

"Is that such a bad thing?"

I shrugged. My father always had connections like that, so I guess I wasn't surprised when he told me that. We sat there and stared at each other for a moment, silence filling the air in the room.

"There are plenty of self-made millionaires in the world under the age of thirty-five. Why me?" he asked.

127

"How the hell do I know? All my boss told me was they took a poll and you were one of the top two."

"Who else was on the list?"

"Craig Pines, owner of Rosie's in Los Angeles."

"Really? I've eaten there. Excellent food. So that's why you were in Los Angeles. You interviewed him. Didn't you?"

"I did."

"And how did that go?"

"It went great. Craig was very open and accommodating," I replied in a smug tone.

"I bet he was." A sly smirk crossed his face.

My legs wouldn't stop trembling no matter how hard I tried to make them. They definitely remembered what it felt like to be wrapped around his muscular body.

"Okay, Mr. Coleman, why don't we get down to business?"

"You can call me Wyatt." He smiled. "As much as I would love to get down to business with you, I'm afraid I can't. I have a meeting in about ten minutes that I need to be at. Are you still staying at that Airbnb you were so excited about?"

"No. I checked out of there this morning."

"Then where are you staying?"

"The Surrey."

"Ah. Expensive taste. The *Seattle Times* sure pays a pretty penny for their employee's travels."

"Eric, my boss, isn't happy about it, but I do as I please."

"Yes, I get that impression. I'll tell you what, I'll pick you up at your hotel around eight o'clock for dinner and we'll

The Interview: New York & Los Angeles

discuss things. Maybe you can persuade me to do an interview after all." He smirked.

My legs tightened, for I knew damn well what he meant.

"If you're insinuating that I need to have sex with you to get the interview, you're sadly mistaken, Wyatt."

"Coming from the girl who fucked a total stranger in the airport." He grinned.

"That was a one-time thing." I pointed at him. "We weren't supposed to see each other again."

"But we have, twice now. We'll discuss it more later over dinner." He got up from his chair, walked over to me, and extended his hand. I quickly dismissed it because I knew if I placed my hand in his, that would be it.

"Thank you for wanting to help me from my seat, but I'm capable of getting up on my own."

He didn't say word. He just flashed a devilish smile as he walked over and opened his office door.

"After you," he spoke. "By the way, please apologize to my secretary."

"Fine." I rolled my eyes as I walked out of his office.

"Oh, before I head to my meeting, I'm going to need your phone number just in case something comes up."

"Of course you do." I rattled off my number as he put it in his phone and then walked away.

I turned and looked at Tamara, who sat there with a confused look on her face.

"Hi, I'm Laurel Holloway." I extended my hand.

"You're the one who called a few days ago about

interviewing Mr. Coleman." She lightly shook my hand.

"I'm sorry about my little story earlier. I just needed to get in to see him."

"So, what you said wasn't true?"

"No. I've never met him before until now."

"Oh. Okay. Well, I'm happy that was all false."

I headed down the hallway with a smile across my face. What I wanted to tell her was that we indeed did have an encounter, but it was completely mutual and welcomed.

The Interview: New York & Los Angeles

Chapter Twenty

I walked out of the building, grabbed my phone from my purse, and facetimed George.

"Hey there." He smiled.

"Oh my God! You are never going to believe what just happened."

"You got the interview with Wyatt Coleman?"

"I don't know yet. He's taking me to dinner tonight. Sit down."

"Why?"

"George, just sit down!"

"Okay. Okay." He took a seat behind his desk.

"Wyatt Coleman is the man from the plane!"

"Shut the fuck up, Laurel! The one you fucked at the airport and then told off at the ballet?"

"Yes. Imagine the look on my face when he opened his office door."

"Holy shit. What happened?"

"The girl he was with at the ballet is his sister. He took her there as an early birthday present. He told me he doesn't have a girlfriend and is taking me out tonight."

"Why do I get the feeling that he won't give you an interview unless you sleep with him again."

"Exactly, and he kind of hinted at that. Telling me that maybe I can persuade him." I narrowed my eye at my phone.

"Be careful, Laurel. This guy had a real effect on you. Something I've never seen since we were in college."

"I know. I'm not having sex with him. He can forget it. I hated myself and how I felt after the first time. That person wasn't me."

"If you want my honest opinion, I believe it was you. He brought out feelings in you that you buried so deep all those years ago."

"Whatever, George. We had sex one time and that was it. You can't develop feelings for someone after one time."

"I hate to break the news to you, darling, but you can, and you did. Don't try to backtrack now or deny it."

"Ugh." I put my hand up to the screen.

"Where are you walking to?"

I looked around. "I don't know." I laughed. "I still have the day, so I think I'm going to do some shopping. Maybe find a new dress for dinner tonight."

"Put it on the company card." He grinned. "It's all for business. You need to look sexy to get that interview."

"Good idea! I'll need you to back me up when Eric threatens to fire me."

"No problem." He laughed. "Listen, I have to go. Call me tonight after you get back to the hotel and let me know how it went. If I don't hear from you, I'll know you spent the night

The Interview: New York & Los Angeles

with him."

"I'm not going to."

"We'll see." He smirked. "Love you."

"Love you too."

I made my way to Bloomingdales and found the perfect dress for tonight. An asymmetrical ruffled sleeveless dress that sat above the knee in a color called Nautilus. It wasn't too fancy or too casual. The best part was that the black stilettos I was wearing earlier matched perfectly. As I was sitting in the back of the cab on the way to the hotel, my phone dinged with a text message from an unfamiliar number.

"Looking forward to seeing you this evening. In case you haven't figured it out, this is Wyatt."

"Considering you're the only person who has asked me out for tonight, I knew it was you. I'm looking forward to getting that interview."

"Is the interview all you're thinking about? Because I'm thinking about other things we're going to do."

"Aren't you just a horny little devil. How long has it been since your cock has been buried deep inside a woman's warm and wet pussy?"

I grinned as I hit the send button.

"Fuck, Laurel. Stop it. I'm in a meeting and now my cock is rock hard."

"You started it, big guy. I'll see you at eight. Don't be late. If there's one thing I can't stand about a person is their inability to arrive on time for something. And by the way, you might want to put that hand to good use before you pick me up."

He didn't respond, but I didn't expect him to. When I arrived back at the hotel, I hung my dress in the closet, kicked off my shoes, and lay down on the bed. Just as I shut my eyes for a quick nap, my phone rang, and it was Eric.

"WHAT!" I answered.

"Excuse me, but why are you lying on the bed? Shouldn't you be at Mr. Coleman's office getting that interview?"

"I was already there. It turns out that Mr. Coleman is the man from the airport."

"The one you had sex with?"

"Yes."

"Excellent work, Laurel. You'll be getting that interview. But why aren't you still at his office?"

"He had a meeting. He's picking me up at eight o'clock for dinner."

"Good. Am I to assume you aren't flying back to Seattle tomorrow?"

"I don't know yet. It all depends on how things go tonight."

"Well, just so we're clear, I'm expecting you back here on Wednesday. So, work your magic tonight."

I rolled my eyes. "I need to go. My anxiety is in full swing right now."

"You don't have anxiety, Laurel."

"You know what, Eric, you're right. But I do seem to get it every time your face appears on my phone screen. Now, I need to nap." I hit the end button.

I lay there, staring up at the ceiling while visions of Wyatt played in my head. What the hell was it about that man I couldn't get off my mind? Maybe it was the way he was so confident. He was so sure of himself and not afraid to show it.

The Interview: New York & Los Angeles

I first noticed it that day at the airport when he led me to the bathroom and again in his office. As sexy as he was, he lost a couple points for accusing me of stalking him.

Chapter Twenty-One

It was seven fifty-five when I turned off the light in the bathroom and slipped into my stiletto heels. I was curious to see if Mr. Coleman would be on time. If not, he'd lose another point. Seven fifty-nine and there was knock at the door. My belly started to flutter as I walked over and opened it, trying to hide the gulp that erupted in the back of my throat when I saw sexy godly man standing there.

"Damn. You're sexy." He grinned as his eyes devoured me from head to toe.

"Thank you. You're looking mighty fine yourself there, handsome." I smirked. "Come on in."

"Thanks. Are you ready?" he asked as he stepped inside.

"I just have to grab my purse. Where are we going?"

"I made a reservation at Marea. I hope you like Italian and seafood."

"I love Italian and seafood." I smiled as I grabbed my purse from the desk.

He opened the door for me, and when I stepped out into the hallway, he took hold of my arm and wrapped it around his. I glanced at him with an arch in my brow.

"What? I want everyone to know you're mine, at least for

tonight." He winked.

My belly did a triple flip and my heart added a few extra beats. This was going to be a long night. We stepped out of the hotel and there was a black limousine waiting at the curb.

"Yours?" I asked.

"Of course."

His driver opened the door and I climbed inside and Wyatt scooted in next to me. The privacy window was up, so I lightly tapped on it.

"Yes, ma'am?"

"I'm Laurel, and you are?"

"Ryan."

"It's nice to meet you, Ryan."

"You as well." He nodded before putting the window back up.

"Was that necessary?" Wyatt asked.

"Was what necessary?"

"Introducing yourself to my driver."

"Of course, it was. Frankly, it was rude of you not to do it yourself."

"Are you always this outspoken?" His eye narrowed at me.

"Yes, I am." The corners of my mouth curved upwards.

"I didn't feel it was necessary to introduce you to him."

"Why not?"

"I don't know. Why are you making this a big deal?"

"Because Ryan is a person too. He's not just your driver and he should be introduced to those who ride in your vehicle. My father used to do the same thing and it drove me insane."

"Your father had a driver?"

"Yes. He still does. His name is Franklin and he's super sweet."

"And what exactly does your father do for a living?"

"Owns and operates Holloway Capital."

The look on his face turned to shock.

"You're kidding me. You're the daughter of Jefferson Holloway?"

"One of his daughters. Why do you look so shocked?"

"Holloway Capital is a major financer for a lot of our projects."

"I'm not surprised."

"I've met with your father on several occasions. Why aren't you working for him?" he asked as the limo stopped in front of the restaurant.

"Because I've always wanted to be a journalist. Plus, I need to be as far away from my family as possible."

As soon as we were seated, our waiter walked over to the table and filled our glasses with water.

"Good evening, Mr. Coleman. It's a pleasure to see you again."

"Good evening, Jean. This beautiful woman sitting across from me is Laurel Holloway."

"Good evening, Miss Holloway." He nodded.

The Interview: New York & Los Angeles

"Good evening, Jean." I smiled.

"May I start you off with a glass of wine?" he asked.

"We'll have a bottle of your 1983 Dom Perignon P3 Moet & Chandon," Wyatt replied.

"Excellent choice, sir. I'll get that right away for you."

"I'd say 'excellent choice' too at twenty-seven hundred dollars a bottle," I spoke.

"A beautiful woman deserves only the finest champagne." He smiled.

"I love how you're trying to butter me up for sex. Did your hand get a good workout today?" I smirked.

"Like I said earlier, outspoken. You seem to be very interested in my hand wrapped around my cock. Maybe later I'll have to perform for you."

Jesus, the thought made my panties wet. Time for a subject change or I was going to jump across the table and devour him. Jean walked over to our table, poured our champagne, and then took our order.

"That won't be necessary." I took a sip of my drink. "So, I'm going to get down to the nitty gritty of things. Why is a man like you still single? It's obvious you can have any woman you want."

"True. I can have any woman I want, and that's the point. Why settle for one flower when you can have your very own garden full of them?" He held up his glass.

Wow. In all the years that I've met, known, and dated men, I'd never run across someone like Wyatt Coleman. I sat there with an arch in my brow as I stared at him.

"What? It's the truth. Now it's my turn. Why is someone like you single? You're absolutely gorgeous, strong-willed, and career-oriented. What's your story, Miss Holloway? Why hasn't some man snatched you up?" His eye narrowed.

Jean, our waiter, walked over to our table and set our plates down in front of us.

"I hope your champagne is satisfactory," he spoke to Wyatt.

"Ask Miss Holloway her thoughts." He smirked.

Jean turned his eyes over to me.

"The champagne is wonderful, Jean." I gave a light nod.

"Very good. I'll be back to check on you soon."

After he walked away, Wyatt picked up his fork.

"You haven't answered my question yet."

"First of all, I don't let any man snatch me up. And second, I'm single because **I'M** my favorite person." I smiled.

"Perhaps you are, but I sense a deep-rooted issue with you and men. You boldly told me off at the ballet because you saw me with my sister and you thought she was either my wife or my girlfriend. You thought I cheated and it struck a nerve with you or else you wouldn't have bothered. Then you bravely told me that you hated men who cheat. So, I'm going with someone broke your heart and you haven't been able to trust ever since. Am I right?"

Damn him.

"As a matter of fact, you are right. Two men in my lifetime have broken my heart: my college boyfriend and my father."

"I'm sorry about that," he spoke.

"One cheated on me and the other consistently cheats on my mother. I'm sure now you can understand why I reacted the way I did when I saw you with your sister."

The Interview: New York & Los Angeles

"I think I can understand."

"How about you? How many broken hearts have you had in your life?"

He reached for his glass and brought it up to his lips, taking a sip before answering my question.

"Zero."

I let out a light laugh. "You're telling me no one has ever broken your heart?"

"Yes. Unless you count Kimmy Trello when I was eight years old."

"And what did eight-year-old Kimmy Trello do that broke your heart? Break one of your toys?" I smirked.

"Kimmy Trello wasn't eight; she was sixteen and she was my babysitter."

"Now that's creepy."

"She had a boyfriend, and every time she babysat me, he was with her. Broke my heart in two seeing them together." The corners of his mouth slightly curved into a cunning smile.

"So, you're telling me she's the reason why you need a garden full of flowers instead of a single one?"

"No, not at all. It's just what I prefer. Being in a relationship is a huge gamble and trying to find a woman who's worth the risk is exhausting. I'm a very busy man and I don't like to waste time. Especially time I don't have. Who wants or has time for break ups, countless trying, or divorce? The last thing I want to do is to hurt someone because I can't or won't commit to them. I like to keep my options open. I don't want to have any worries or cares when I'm out or on a business trip and meet someone else. I'm very upfront with the women I date. They know the risk in going out with me. I don't make it a secret."

Chapter Twenty-Two

I sat there, listened to every word he spoke, and took it all in.

"And what risk is that?" I asked.

"If they fall in love with me or become emotionally attached, it's on them and unrequited."

I had to give the man props for being brutally honest. Honesty was rare these days when it came to men. He had given me some information for the article without realizing it. But how I was going to write it without making him sound like too much of a narcissistic douchebag was going to be tricky. I needed more.

"With Craig Pines, I did a day in the life. If you wouldn't mind, I'd like to do that with you."

"Exactly what does that consist of?"

"I'd follow you around for a couple of days. Get a glimpse of your work life and what you like to do in your free time."

"I don't know about that. You're fully aware I don't do interviews."

"Oh come on, Wyatt. You're thirty-two years old and a billionaire. Give people a glimpse into your life. You may inspire someone. Even if you inspired only one person, it's so worth it."

The Interview: New York & Los Angeles

"*Forbes Magazine* did a brief business article on me a couple of years ago. People already know about me."

"*Forbes.*" I waved my hand in front of my face. "That's so boring and mostly read by men. My article is geared towards women. Women want to know about you. You're in their fantasies. Give them a little more to fantasize about."

"And what do I get out of this deal?" he asked.

"Knowing that you made a woman's day?"

"I know that every day. I don't need to have an article written about my personal life to give me that. For example, I know I made your day when we arrived in New York." A smirk crossed his lips.

"Mental note. This guy is full of himself," I spoke with a narrowed eye.

"Oh come on, Laurel. Just admit it. The orgasms, the way your skin trembles under my touch, and the sexual moans that escaped your lips with every thrust of my cock."

I tightened my legs under the table. He was doing this on purpose. I started to sweat as I tried to ignore the pulsating vibrations down below. Picking up my glass of water, I gulped it, trying to cool myself down.

"We're not talking about that. We're talking about you doing an interview for my magazine."

"I know you're thinking about it." A sexy smirk crossed his face.

"The only thing I'm thinking about is getting this interview and getting back on a plane to Seattle." I finished the last of my champagne.

"Let me sleep on it. I'll let you know in the morning." He winked.

"Is there anything else I can get for the two of you?" Jean asked.

"We're all set, Jean. We'll be having dessert somewhere else," he expressed as the corners of his mouth slightly curved upwards.

He slipped his credit card into the billfold, and when Jean came back, Wyatt left a generous tip and signed on the dotted line. We both got up from our seats, and as we were walking through the restaurant towards the doors, I felt his hand on the small of my back. I took in a deep breath. He was right, I trembled every time he touched me. The limo pulled up to the curb of the hotel. As soon as Wyatt climbed out, he held out his hand to me. Placing mine in his, I once again trembled as a shot of electricity soared through my body.

"Thank you for dinner," I spoke as I stared into his eyes.

He brought the back of his hand to my cheek and lightly stroked it.

"You're welcome. I hope you enjoyed it."

"I did. It was delicious." My skin shrouded itself in goosebumps.

He leaned in and softly brushed his lips against mine. One light brush became two and two became three. Before I knew it, we were locked in a passionate kiss, our tongues tangling in the night.

"Go get a room, you two," a passerby snarled.

I broke our kiss and let out a light laugh.

"You do have a room here," Wyatt spoke.

"I do, don't I? Would you like to come up for a drink?"

"I was hoping you'd ask." He grinned.

He held out his arm and I hooked mine around it as we walked inside and headed to the elevators. Once we arrived at my room, I pulled my key card from my purse and slid into the lock. We barely made it inside before he had me in his grip, shut the door, and pinned me up against it, his mouth on mine. His hand slid up my dress and his fingers deftly caressed my wet opening.

"My God. You aren't wearing any underwear," he spoke breathlessly.

"Nope. Decided to go commando tonight."

"Fuck. That's so hot." His mouth smashed against mine while his finger dipped inside me.

I gasped, and his lips went to my neck, his tongue sliding along my earlobe sending such strong vibrations down below I was almost positive an orgasm was about to erupt. I moaned as his finger explored me. God, how I'd thought about this ever since that day at the airport. I reached for his belt and he pulled my hand away and pinned my arm above my head.

"We have plenty of time for that after you come for me."

He firmly placed his thumb on my clit and moved it around in circles while his finger was still inside me, hitting the spot that would send any woman over the edge of eternity. My skin was heated, and my heart was pounding out of my chest. My body was on the brink of exploding and I was pretty sure that I'd die when it did. But I didn't care. At least I'd die a happy woman.

"Oh God. Oh God," I panted.

"Let it go, sweetheart. Give me what I want."

One. Two. Three. My legs stiffened and my body spasmed as a howl erupted from me.

"Perfect." He smiled as he brushed his lips against mine.

"You have no idea how much it turns me on to watch you have an orgasm."

"Keep giving them and I'll keep turning you on," I spoke breathlessly.

He reached behind me and unzipped the zipper to my dress, letting it fall to the ground as he let go of my arm. He took my naked breasts in his grip and fondled them with pleasure, softly stroking my hardened nipples as he stared into my eyes.

"Stay right where you're at and don't move. I want to fuck you up against the door. But first, I want to give you what you've been thinking about all day."

He took a few steps back and unbuttoned his shirt, sliding it off his broad shoulders and tossing it to the ground. His hands went for his belt. I stood there, watching every moment as if it was in slow motion. He removed a condom from his wallet, took down his pants and boxers, and kicked them to the side. His hand wrapped around his hard cock and he slowly started to stroke himself, his eyes never leaving mine. I gulped. I had never been so turned on in my life.

"Is this what you wanted to see?" he asked in a low voice.

I couldn't speak, so I nodded.

"Does it turn you on to watch me masturbate in front of you?"

He slowly started to walk towards me while his hand moved up and down his shaft. I was going to orgasm again just watching him. He stood in front of me, took my hand, wrapped it around his and began stroking himself once again.

"What do you want me to do with this?" he asked in a low and sexy voice.

"Fuck me, Wyatt."

"It would give me great pleasure, but first, get down on your knees and take me in your mouth for a few minutes. But don't make me come."

I got down on my knees, my shoes still on, and wrapped my lips around him, taking him in inch by inch. Sexual groans escaped him as he stroked my hair.

"Okay. That's enough. I won't come this way. Stand up," he commanded.

I stood with my back against the door, one foot up, the heel of my stiletto pressing against it. He tore the condom package open with his mouth and rolled it over his cock. Grabbing my waist with one hand, he pulled my leg around him and thrust inside me. I gasped for air, and after a couple of more thrusts, he pulled out, turned me around, and took me from behind, placing both of his hands firmly on mine, which were pressed against the door. It only took a few pumps to throw me into another orgasm.

"Oh my God," he whispered in my ear as he came to a halt and strained inside me.

I stood there, his heated body pushed against mine as his fingers interlaced with mine. His hot exhausted breath swept across me as we both tried to regain normal breathing.

"That was so fucking good," he spoke before pressing his lips against my shoulder.

"It sure was."

He pulled out of me and I turned around. After removing the condom and throwing it in the trash can, he grabbed his clothes from the floor and took them over to the bed. Reaching into the closet that was right next to me, I pulled a white robe from the hanger and slipped it on.

"Are you leaving?" I asked.

"Yes." He pulled on his pants.

Disappointment shrouded me, but I couldn't let him know.

"Okay. So—"

He buttoned up his shirt, and as he was tucking it into his pants, he stared at me.

"I want to read the article on Craig Pines."

"Why?" I asked in confusion.

"Just to get a feel for your writing. If I like the article, I'll grant you a day in the life. Deal?"

"Uh. Sure. I can send it to you."

"I'll text you my email address when I get in the car." He walked over to me and pressed his warm lips against my forehead. "Tonight was great. I hope you enjoyed it as much as I did."

"I did. Thank you." My lips formed a small smile.

He walked out the door, the loud bang when it closed, jolted me. I went into the bathroom, placed my hands firmly on the sink, and looked into the mirror. Shaking my head, I pointed to myself. "Don't. Don't you dare, Laurel."

I could hear the email tone come through on my phone, so I walked over to my purse and retrieved it, staring at the email address Wyatt Coleman sent me. Grabbing my laptop, I sat on the bed, pulled up the article on Craig Pines, and sent it to him.

The Interview: New York & Los Angeles

Chapter Twenty-Three

I was looking over the questions for Everything Laurel when a text message from Wyatt came through.

"I liked the article, even though I suspect you left some things out of it. Just a hunch. Ryan will be by the hotel to pick you up at seven a.m. You got your day in the life, Miss Holloway."

"Yes!" I shouted in excitement.

"I'll be ready. Thank you, Wyatt."

"You can thank me tomorrow night. I have a fundraiser to attend and you'll be attending with me."

"Sounds fun."

"Good night, Laurel."

"Good night, Wyatt."

I glanced at the time and it was already midnight, nine o'clock in Seattle. I needed to text Eric to let him know that I would be staying in New York a couple more days.

"It's me! I'm doing a day in the life of Wyatt Coleman starting tomorrow morning. So, I'm going to need a couple of more days here."

"Good job. But you better check out of that hotel, then. I'm

149

not paying for another night there. Your couple of days turns into a week."

"I'm not checking out and I'll pay for the remaining days I'm here myself."

"Be my guest. Keep me posted."

I stuck my tongue out at my phone and then set it on the nightstand. Pulling the covers over me, I laid there and stared up at the ceiling as the events of tonight haunted me. When I closed my eyes, I only saw him. His smile, his laughter, his naked body.

The next morning, I was up early and down to the lobby at precisely six fifty-five. A black limo pulled up to the curb and Ryan got out and opened the door for me.

"Good morning, Miss Holloway." He nodded.

"Good morning, Ryan, and please, just Laurel."

He gave me a pleasant smile, and as I slid into the backseat, the smell of clean earthy and musky scents smacked me in the face.

"Good morning." Wyatt grinned.

"Good morning. I didn't think you'd be in the car."

"Why not? You want a day in the life, so it starts on our way to the office."

"What exactly does Coleman Enterprises do?" I curiously asked.

"It's obvious you didn't do your research prior to trying to secure an interview."

"What can I say? I like to be surprised."

"I buy failing companies, get them back on track, and then

The Interview: New York & Los Angeles

sell them to the highest bidder."

"May I ask how you got started?"

"My grandfather started Coleman Enterprises thirty years ago. When he passed away, my sister and I took over."

"What about your father?"

"I never knew the dirt bag. He left my mom when I was two, shortly after my sister was born."

"I'm sorry."

"Don't be." The corners of his mouth curved into a sexy smile. "We were better off without him. My grandfather was a father to me and Sammi."

As soon as we climbed out of the limo, we took the elevator up to Coleman Enterprises and I followed Wyatt down the hall to his office.

"Good morning, Tamara," he spoke.

"Yes. Good morning, Tamara." I grinned.

"Good morning, Mr. Coleman. Miss Holloway."

"Laurel will be following me around today. I've agreed to let her to do a day in the life for her magazine article. Let's accommodate her the best we can."

"Not a problem, sir."

I followed Wyatt into his office and took a seat in the chair across from his desk.

"I have a couple of meetings scheduled, but I'm afraid you're not allowed in them. So, you can go shop for a new dress for the fundraiser tonight. I'll have Tamara give you the company card since you'll be attending with me."

"I have a dress," I spoke.

"If you're talking about the dress you wore to the ballet, and as beautiful as you looked in it, it's not formal enough."

"Oh. Then I guess I will have to go shopping."

"Hey, Wyatt." His office door opened. "Sorry. I didn't know you were in a meeting."

"Sammi, come in. I want you to meet Miss Laurel Holloway. She's going to interview me for a magazine article."

"How the hell did you manage that?" She smiled as she walked over and extended her hand.

"Laurel, this is my sister, Sammi Coleman."

"It's nice to meet you, Miss Coleman." I lightly shook her hand.

"Please, call me Sammi. I hate formalities. Wyatt, everything is set for the fundraiser tonight and there will be approximately five hundred guests attending."

"Excellent. Thanks, sis."

"You're welcome. Now, if you'll excuse me, I have a bagel sitting in my office that is calling my name. It was nice to meet you, Laurel."

"You too."

I sat there with a narrowed eye, staring at Wyatt as he turned on his computer.

"What's that look for?" he asked with an arch in his brow.

"The fundraiser I'm attending with you, you're the one putting it on?"

"I am. Why?"

"Why didn't you tell me that in the first place? All you said was that you were attending a fundraiser and I was going with

The Interview: New York & Los Angeles

you."

"And?" He cocked his head.

"The appropriate thing to have said was, 'I'm putting on a fundraiser tonight and I would like you to attend with me.'"

"I'm still attending it. What does it matter if I'm putting it on?"

Irritation filled me as I put my hand up.

"Forget it. What is this fundraiser for?"

The corners of his mouth curved upwards into a cunning smile.

"I'm messing with you and I apologize. I should have told you from the start that I was the one hosting it. Anyway, it's for MS."

"Multiple Sclerosis?" I asked.

"Yes. My mother was crippled with it for years. Her suffering ended a year ago when she passed away from a heart attack."

"Wyatt. I'm sorry."

"Thank you. I appreciate it. This is the third annual MS fundraiser. I want a cure found so people who have it don't have to suffer like my mother did. Now, if you'll excuse me, I have my first meeting of the day. We'll talk later."

"Okay." I smiled.

Chapter Twenty-Four

After he walked out, I went over to the large dark cherry wood bookcase that filled one wall and examined all the books that sat upon it. Most of them were books about business, but he had a few that caught my attention. *Moby Dick* and *The Great Gatsby* sat in between the works of Shakespeare, William Blake, and Charles Dickens. His degree was from Harvard, framed in a dark wood that sat one shelf below.

I walked out of his office and stood at Tamara's desk, waiting for her to get off the phone.

"I'm sorry, Miss Jones, but I've already told you that Mr. Coleman is in a meeting. I have no idea why he hasn't called you back. Yes. I will give him the message as soon as he returns. Goodbye." She sighed as she placed the phone on the receiver.

"I take it Miss Jones is a pain in the ass?" I arched my brow.

"Seems that way."

"Scorned lover perhaps?" I gave a cocky smile.

"To be honest, Laurel, I have no idea. She kind of sounded like it. She's called about twenty times over the past few days."

"Do you deal with these situations quite often?" I asked as I took a seat on the edge of her desk.

"More times than I'd like to."

The Interview: New York & Los Angeles

"And what does Wyatt say?"

"He tells me to ignore them. But that's kind of hard to do when they keep calling the office because he doesn't return phone calls or text messages. God, please don't tell him I told you that."

"No worries. I'm not surprised anyway. Since he's in a meeting, I'm going to go grab some coffee and then get a dress for the fundraiser tonight."

"Oh. That reminds me." She opened her desk drawer. "Mr. Coleman asked me to give this to you."

"Perfect." I grinned. "Who am I to turn down a free dress?"

I hailed a cab to Nordstrom. I know. I was in New York, fashion capital of the world, and I chose one of the most basic stores. The truth was, if I ever needed a formal dress, Nordstrom was my go-to store. I didn't want to spend all day shopping and I knew I'd find something there. As soon as I entered the store, I went straight to the women's dress section, and low and behold, the perfect dress was beautifully displayed on a mannequin. A black embroidered fitted long dress with spaghetti straps that crossed in the back and a princess-seamed bodice with gold beads and embroidery. I finally found the rack where the dress hung and anxiously slid each hanger across the steel bar trying to find a small. *Shit*. All they had left were mediums. Glancing over at the mannequin, I stood there biting down on my lower lip, knowing damn well that dress was the size I needed. I looked around for a sales associate. No one seemed to be around, so I took it upon myself to get the dress.

As I was standing on the platform, undressing the mannequin without a care in the world, I heard a voice.

"Excuse me. What do you think you're doing?"

"This is the size I need and you didn't have any on the rack," I spoke as I successfully removed the dress and the arm of the mannequin along with it. "Oops."

"Customers are not allowed to do what you just did. We have a policy."

"If you're talking about breaking the arm off, I apologize. It was an accident. But if you're talking about removing the dress from the mannequin, then maybe one of you sales associates should have been available to help me. I looked around and no one was to be found anywhere. Now, I would like to try this on, please." I smiled at her.

"I'm sorry, but I can't let you do that. The dress is for the mannequin. If you need a small and we don't have any on the floor, I will be happy to order it for you. Free of charge, of course."

"I need this dress for tonight, so ordering it won't be possible. May I ask your name?"

"Becca." She glared at me.

"You seem like a really nice woman, Becca, and I know you're following policy. Which, by the way, is a stupid policy and I'd like to see it in writing. I'm the customer, this dress is my size, and I would like to try it on."

"And your name?" she asked.

"Laurel Holloway, reporter for the *Seattle Times*. Gosh, my head is just spinning right now with words for the article I feel the need to write about this store and my experience. Plus, I'll have to tell Mr. Wyatt Coleman about my experience here since he sent me to buy this specific dress. Wait," I pulled out my phone, "let me call and tell him that you're refusing to let me try this lovely dress on."

"That won't be necessary, Miss Holloway." She took the dress and led me into the fitting room. "If you need anything else, please let me know."

"Thank you." I smirked.

The Interview: New York & Los Angeles

I looked at myself in the full-length mirror and the dress was perfect. Picking up my phone from the chair, I facetimed George.

"Hello. Whoa, sexy dress!"

"Do you love?"

"I do. What's it for?"

"I'm attending a fundraiser tonight put on by Mr. Wyatt Coleman himself for MS."

"It's perfect, Laurel."

"Thanks. I have to run now and get back to Wyatt's office."

"When are you coming home?" He pouted.

"Soon. I promise. Love you."

"Love you too. Have fun tonight."

"Thanks." I blew him a kiss and ended the call.

After changing back into my regular clothes, I grabbed the dress and took it up to the sales counter.

"Will this be all?" Becca asked.

"Yes."

She handed me the dress, and as I was walking out of the dress area, I saw Sammi, Wyatt's sister, standing there with a smile on her face.

"Sammi, what are you doing here?"

"Some last-minute shopping. I think I officially love you." She grinned.

"Why?" I laughed.

"I was across the way when I saw you undressing the

mannequin and that sales associate walked up to you. I heard the whole thing. You're good, Laurel."

"Thanks." I smiled.

We rode back to Coleman Enterprises together, and when I approached Wyatt's office, I found him sitting behind his desk sipping from a white mug.

"Is that coffee in there or something stronger?"

"Coffee." He grinned. "You found a dress."

"I did."

"Can I take a look?"

"Sure. When it's on me tonight and when you come to pick me up." I smirked.

"I was thinking about that. Since you're going to be here a couple of more days and your boss is throwing a tantrum about the hotel bill, why don't you stay free of charge at my place?"

"Seriously? You want me to stay with you?" I raised my brow.

"Yes. You're writing an article about me. Why not? I have several spare rooms, but you'll be staying in mine."

"So free of charge really isn't the deal. You expect sex as payment?"

"I don't look at it that way, but if you do." He shrugged.

"Fine. I'll stay at your place."

"Good. I'll have Ryan take you to your hotel, so you can collect your things."

"Now?" I asked.

"Yeah. I have two more meetings today and I'm not sure

The Interview: New York & Los Angeles

how long they're going to last. You'll just be bored here."

"Okay, then I'm off. Is Ryan downstairs?"

"Yes. I'll let him know you're coming. I'll see you later." He winked before planting a kiss on my forehead.

"Oh, by the way, you better call Miss Jones back and stop putting your secretary through hell with your douchebag man ways."

He stood there with a smirk on his face and slowly shook his head.

A tingling sensation invaded my entire body, my belly flipped about a hundred times, and my heart rate was up. I took in a deep breath as I walked out of his office.

Chapter Twenty-Five

Ryan pulled up to 425 West 50th Street, grabbed my luggage, and took me up to Penthouse D on the top floor.

"Fancy." I smiled as the elevator doors opened and I stepped inside the foyer. I didn't expect anything less from Wyatt.

"Mr. Coleman instructed that I put your bags in his room."

"Yes, he did insist I stay with him. Listen, Ryan. How many other women has Wyatt done this with?"

"Done what?"

"Temporarily moved a woman into his place."

"Never. You're the first." A smile greeted his lips.

"Really?"

"Yes. I will say that I was quite shocked when he called and told me. This is something Mr. Coleman doesn't do."

That tingly feeling invaded me again.

"It's just because I'm writing that article on him."

"If you say so." He nodded. "Laurel, I hope I'm not overstepping, but I don't want to see you get hurt. I like you, but Mr. Coleman—"

"It's okay, Ryan. I know all about Mr. Coleman, and to be

The Interview: New York & Los Angeles

honest, he can't hurt me. I'm the same as him. I don't get involved. I just like to have a little fun."

"Very well. Mr. Coleman said to make yourself at home. If there's anything you need, just call."

"Thank you, Ryan."

"You're welcome."

As soon as he left the penthouse, I explored. The kitchen featured Smallbone of Devizes cabinetry with solid European oak frames. How did I know? They were the same cabinets my mother put into our house and wouldn't stop talking about for the first year. Polished concrete countertops fit in perfectly as well as the Waterwork fixtures and Miele appliances. The windowed kitchen led directly to a massive great room with two balconies, one facing east and one facing west with a wood-burning fireplace. The walls throughout the house were a light gray color with furniture in a darker gray. The dining room housed a table that seated six with an elegant fireplace and floor-to-ceiling windows.

I went upstairs and took the long hallway to the master suite. A mixture of light and dark grays saturated the space. He sure did love his grays. Who was I to judge since my apartment was filled with grays as well. After my shower, I stood in front of the bathroom mirror wrapped in a towel and applied my makeup. Suddenly, my phone rang, and Eric's face appeared.

"Hello, Eric."

"Did you just get out of the shower or something?"

"Yes. Hence the reason why my body and hair are wrapped in towels."

"What are you doing? Shouldn't you be with Wyatt Coleman? Wait. Where are you? That's not your hotel room. Laurel, I swear to God."

"Chill out, Eric. I'm at Wyatt's penthouse and I'm getting ready to attend the fundraiser with him tonight."

"Why are you there?"

"Because he asked me to stay with him a couple of days for the article."

"Good. Less expense on the company's part."

I rolled my eyes.

"You're sleeping with him still, aren't you?"

"So, what if I am? He's single. I'm single. No harm."

"Don't get attached, Laurel."

"Please, Eric. Do you not know me by now?"

"Just be careful. I don't need you coming back here all out of sorts."

"Are we done? You caught me in the middle of makeup."

"Two days, Laurel, and I want you back in Seattle and sitting behind your desk writing that article. It's not up for discussion anymore."

"Fine. I'll be back in two days." I hit the end button.

A funny feeling erupted in the pit of my stomach. A feeling I didn't like. After my hair and makeup were done, I slipped into my new dress.

"Look at you." Wyatt smiled as he walked into his bedroom. "Damn. You're going to be the sexiest woman there."

"Stop." I pretended to blush. "I bet you say that to all the girls." I put my hand out and he grabbed it.

"Actually, I don't." He pressed his lips against my skin. "I heard you took it upon yourself to undress the mannequin at

The Interview: New York & Los Angeles

Nordstrom," he spoke as he unbuttoned his shirt.

"Sammi told you?"

"Yeah. She said you were fierce with the sales associate."

"She was being ridiculous," I spoke as I put on my earrings.

"I get the impression you're the type of woman who always gets what she wants."

"I do ninety-nine percent of the time. By the way, nice place you have here. Very prestigious."

He walked into the bathroom in nothing but his silk boxers and a roaring ache hit me down below. His muscular back was just as sexy as the rest of him.

"Thanks. My grandfather gave it to me when I started working for his company. He did the same for my sister. She lives one floor below. He was a firm believer that family needs to stay close."

"He sounds like he was a good man." I gently smiled.

"He was, and I miss him. I'm going to finish getting ready. I should only be about fifteen minutes. If you want, there's a bottle of wine in the fridge."

"Sounds good. I'll meet you downstairs."

****

The moment we entered *360*, a prestigious venue in the heart of Tribeca, Wyatt made his rounds welcoming the generous guests that had already arrived. This was impressive. I'd heard about this venue but never actually had been here. It was stunning. All thirty-thousand square feet of it. I excused myself from Wyatt and headed over to the bar.

"What can I get you?"

"I'll have a neat martini, straight up with two olives."

"Coming right up." The young and cute bartender smiled.

I pulled my phone from my clutch and dialed my father.

"Laurel, what a nice surprise," he answered.

"Hey, Dad."

"Where are you? It sounds noisy."

"I'm still in New York at a fundraiser that Mr. Coleman is hosting."

"Wyatt Coleman? I didn't know you knew him."

"He's the man I was sent to interview for the magazine. I was hoping Holloway Capital could make a generous donation."

"What's the fundraiser for, pumpkin?"

"MS."

"Ah. Of course. I'll do it right now."

"Thanks, Dad."

"How about coming home for a couple of days after you leave New York?"

"As much as I'd love to, I'm afraid I can't. Eric wants me back in Seattle in a couple of days."

"Alright. Well, take a weekend and come home soon."

"I'll try, Dad. I have to go. Thanks again for the donation."

"You're welcome, sweetheart. Have fun. Oh, and by the way, don't get too attached to Wyatt Coleman. He's an excellent businessman who knows his stuff, but when it comes to women, he likes to play the field. He's a charmer and I've seen women melt right before my eyes and get their hearts broken."

"I haven't melted yet and I don't plan to," I lied. "I'll talk to you soon."

After ending the call, I looked at my phone in disgust. *Wasn't he the pot calling the kettle black.* Shaking my head, I put my phone away and grabbed the martini the bartender set on the counter.

"Hors d'oeuvre, miss?" A man dressed in a white tux approached me.

"Don't mind if I do. I'm starving." I grinned as I took several.

"You do realize you're only supposed to take one or two of them, right?" Wyatt smirked as he walked over to me. "That's proper etiquette. Something a woman of your stature should know."

"I'm all about breaking etiquette." I shoved a piece of shrimp into my mouth. "Been doing it since I was little just to piss my mother off."

Wyatt chuckled. "I bet you were quite the little rebel back then."

"Still am." I grinned.

Suddenly, a woman with long black hair and dark eyes that sported way too much makeup approached us.

"What the fuck, Wyatt?"

"Adele. What on earth are you doing here?" he asked as he lightly took hold of her arm.

"I'm here in my father's place. He's taken ill and since you refuse to return my text messages and phone calls, I decided to take his place. Who the hell is this?" She glared at me from head to toe. "One of your whores you're going to screw over next?"

"That's enough, Adele."

"Ah, you must be Miss Jones, the woman who was harassing Mr. Coleman's secretary this morning."

"Excuse me?" She placed her hand on her hip.

"Listen, sweetheart. First of all, I'm not a whore. Yes, I'm here with Mr. Coleman, but it's strictly on a professional level."

"So, you're a prostitute? High-class call girl? What? Is he paying you to have sex with him?"

"Adele, I'm going to have you escorted out of here in two seconds if you don't stop," Wyatt scowled.

"Go ahead, Wyatt, and that means my father's check goes with me."

"It's okay, Wyatt." I placed my hand on his chest. "Miss Jones, I'm flattered that you think I could be a high-class call girl, but in reality, I'm a reporter for the *Seattle Times* and I'm writing an article on Mr. Coleman. This fundraiser will be mentioned in the article, hence the reason I'm tagging along. Now, I'm sorry that Mr. Coleman hasn't returned any of your calls or text messages, but the truth is he just might not be that into you."

"How dare you," she growled.

"Listen, Adele. I know girls like you. You were born with a silver spoon in your mouth. You're used to getting whatever and whomever you want. Am I right?"

"Yes. Damn straight I am."

"Well, I hate to burst your bubble, princess, but this is one man you'll never get. He doesn't get involved in relationships. He's a fly by the woman kind of guy. He likes his garden full of a variety of flowers. Is that someone you really want to

The Interview: New York & Los Angeles

pursue? My God, woman, have some standards for yourself."

"I have standards!" she shouted.

"Really? Because from what I'm seeing, you don't, or else you wouldn't be going after a man who isn't worthy of your attention. Do you really want to waste your time on someone who will never express his feelings to you or call you his girlfriend? Aren't you worth more than that?"

"Yes, of course I am." She settled down.

"Then stop wasting your precious time on this one." I pointed to Wyatt. "Life is too short to be chasing after the wrong guy who can never give what a woman like you needs and deserves."

"I guess you're right." She reached into her purse, pulled out a check, and handed it to Wyatt. "This is from my father's company. Have a nice life, Wyatt. I can't say that it was a pleasure knowing you."

"Umm, thanks, Adele."

As soon as she walked away, his brows furrowed as he glared at me.

"You're welcome." I smiled as I threw back my drink.

Chapter Twenty-Six

The fundraiser was a huge success, and when the night was over, we went back to Wyatt's penthouse and had incredible sex. Watching him give his speech and radiate the confidence he had turned me on in such a way, it freaked me out.

"Fuck, Laurel," he spoke with bated breath as I collapsed on top of his muscular body.

My lips curled up into a smile as his hands gripped my ass, making sure I didn't move until he was ready for me to.

"I'm sure going to miss this when you leave," he spoke.

"Me too." I grinned as I pressed my lips against his.

He lifted me off him, pulled the condom off, and tossed it in the small trash can next to his bed. He held his arm out, suggesting that I snuggle into him. I did, and I never felt more secure than I did at that moment.

"I'll have to call and thank your father for the generous donation," he spoke as his fingers lightly moved up and down my arm.

"I'm sure he'll appreciate that."

"I should be thanking you because there's no way he would have known about the fundraiser unless you told him."

I lifted my head from his chest and looked at him.

The Interview: New York & Los Angeles

"I did tell him, and you did thank me." I smiled.

"Ah, you considered what we just did a thank you?"

"I do. It's not every day that a woman has one orgasm right after the other." A smirk crossed my face.

"You're easy to please."

I laid my head down, and as I listened to the soft rhythm of his heartbeat, I thought about how I wasn't so easy to please.

"I love your sister," I randomly spoke to change the subject.

"I'm glad. I do too. We're very close."

"I can see that."

"You're not close with your brother and sister?" he asked.

"Not really. I mean, we are in a way, I guess. I always just did my own thing growing up while my mother tended to the two of them."

"It sounds to me like you're jealous of them."

I sat up, covering my naked body with the sheet.

"I'm not jealous of them. Why would you say that?"

"Because it's something I'm picking up on. You moved across the country to get away from your family."

"So? People move across country all the time for work."

"That's true, but I can hear the resentment in your voice every time you talk about your family."

"I came to see my sister perform in the ballet, didn't I?"

"Yes, but I suspect if you didn't have to come to New York to interview me, you wouldn't have."

He was right, and I hated that he was.

"The Holloway's adopted me when they were told they couldn't have children. Two years later, Alfie was born and then came the second surprise, Bella."

"I had no clue you were adopted."

"Things changed when Alfie was born and even more so when Bella arrived. I remember walking down the hallway to my room one night and I heard my mother talking to Bella while she was feeding her. I stopped by the door, which was slightly opened, and listened. She told Bella that she and Alfie were gifts from God and that she had never been happier than when she found out she was pregnant with them." Tears started to form in my eyes. "I don't talk about this shit with anyone." I wiped my eye as I looked away from him.

He brought his hand up to my cheek and softly stroked it.

"It's okay. Maybe this is what you need, Laurel."

"I stood there thinking that I was a gift from God, and that I was born so they could have me. But she never told me that, and once her 'real' children were born, I was pushed to the side. She never made me feel like I was loved equally. She always picked me apart and argued with everything I did. But never with Alfie and Bella. They were perfect in her eyes, no matter what. I remember Alfie hit me in the head with one of his toy trucks because I wouldn't let him play with my toys. I had to get four stitches, and instead of punishing him, my mother told me that I needed to learn to share."

"Where was your father?"

"He worked all the time. We barely saw him. Not only was he building his company, he was building his list of mistresses. Alfie is just like him. Supposedly, he's proposing to his girlfriend, but when he stayed with me at the Airbnb, he was fucking someone else."

"They always say the apple doesn't fall far from the tree," Wyatt spoke.

The Interview: New York & Los Angeles

"Well, this apple who isn't a part of their tree," I pointed to myself, "fell as far away as it could. Like fell, rolled down a hill, and ended up in a field thousands of miles away."

The corners of his mouth curved up into a sexy smile as he let out a chuckle.

"When I was ten years old, I remember overhearing my father on the phone one night in his study. I wasn't feeling good, so I got up to get a drink of water. On my way to the kitchen, I heard him telling someone that he missed her and that he scheduled a business trip and asked her to come with him. Ever since that night, I paid more attention to the way he behaved. When he came home from that business trip, he was as happy as a clam. But after a couple of days, the happiness wore off. It became a pattern, and after a couple of years, my mother suspected. She never told him, though; she just thought an eye for an eye. I was too afraid to ever get in a relationship with a boy because of them. They proved that relationships don't last and that you could never love one person for a lifetime. So, I dated and broke boys' hearts before they could break mine. Then I met David in college, and he made me feel different. I let down my guard and became his girlfriend. Then he cheated on me with my best friend, proving my theory right."

"And what theory is that?" he asked.

"That giving your heart to someone for the rest of your life isn't logical because nothing ever lasts and that nothing in this world is permanent. When two people enter a relationship, it changes them, or at least one of them. You want so badly for the other person to love you that you give up the person you are to become the person you think you should be in order to hold on to them."

"Come here." He pulled me into him and kissed the top of my head. "Let's get some sleep. We can talk more about this in the morning."

"Good idea. I'm exhausted, but we won't be talking about

this again. Good night, Wyatt."

"Good night, Laurel."

I closed my eyes, but instead of falling asleep, my mind became congested with thoughts. Thoughts about Wyatt and how I felt when I was with him, along with thoughts about going back to Seattle. My heart started pounding and my skin became heated. The air in my lungs was constricted and I felt like I was smothering. My body began to shake, and I jumped up and went into the bathroom. Clutching the edge of the sink, I stood there and tried to calm down.

"Laurel, what's wrong?" Wyatt asked as he came up from behind. "My God, you're shaking."

"I'll be fine in a minute."

He stepped out of the bathroom, and a moment later, he returned with a bottle of water. After removing the cap, he held it up to me. I took the bottle from his hands.

"Drink this."

I took a few sips and set the bottle on the counter.

"Thanks. I'm okay. Go back to bed, Wyatt."

"No, Laurel, you're not okay. It looked like you were having a panic attack. What's going on?"

"It was all that talk about my family," I lied. "It stirred up a lot of memories."

"I'm sorry. I never should have asked you about them."

"It's not your fault. Please don't apologize."

He wrapped his arms around me. I was exhausted and all I wanted to do was go to sleep.

"Come on. Let's get you back into bed."

The Interview: New York & Los Angeles

Chapter Twenty-Seven

I opened my eyes as the sunlight peered through the sheer curtains of the bedroom windows. Grabbing my phone from the nightstand, I saw the time was eight a.m.

"Shit."

Climbing out of bed, I slipped on my robe and went downstairs, where I followed the smell of something burning in the kitchen.

"Shouldn't we be at the office? Why didn't you wake me? And what is that smell?"

"Good morning." A sexy smile crossed his lips. "We're not going into the office today. I didn't wake you because you needed to rest, and that smell is the toast I burnt."

He poured me a cup of coffee and handed it to me.

"Thank you. What do you mean we're not going into the office?"

"We're going on a road trip. I need you to go get ready now, so we can stop and grab breakfast first. I thought I had eggs, but I guess I don't and I already burnt the toast. So, it's just best we let someone else take care of breakfast for us."

I couldn't help but let out a light laugh.

"Where are we going?"

"Long Island."

"Why?" I narrowed my eye.

"You'll see when we get there. This will conclude your article on me." He leaned over the island holding his coffee cup between his hands. "Dress comfortably. Jeans, a t-shirt, and tennis shoes if you have any."

"Now you have me really curious, Mr. Coleman."

"Go on. I'll give you about fifteen minutes. I'm starving."

I took an apple from the basket on the counter and tossed it to him.

"I can't promise to be ready in fifteen minutes. I am a woman, you know. This should tide you over in the meantime." I gave him a wink and walked out of the kitchen.

Making my way back up to the bedroom, I picked up my phone and noticed I had a missed call from George. After changing into my clothes, I propped my phone up in the bathroom while I put on some makeup and facetimed him.

"Hey, Laurel."

"I was going to call you later. We need to talk."

"Is everything okay?"

"I had a panic attack last night, here at Wyatt's home, basically in front of him."

"Why? What happened?" he asked with concern.

"I don't know, George. I'm overwhelmed," I spoke with sadness in my voice.

"Oh, Laurel. I knew this day would come eventually."

I heard Wyatt walk into the bedroom.

The Interview: New York & Los Angeles

"I have to go. Wyatt's coming," I whispered before hitting the end button.

"Were you talking to someone?" Wyatt asked.

"My best friend, George. He called earlier, and I missed it."

"You have a gay best friend?"

"George isn't gay. He has a girlfriend whom he's head over heels for."

"Oh. I apologize for being presumptuous. I didn't think guys and girls could be close without any sexual tension in the way."

"They can be. George and I have been best friends since college. I met him the same day I found my ex banging my best friend. We've been stuck together like glue ever since."

"It sounds like he's very important to you."

"He's like a brother to me."

"Are you ready yet? I ate the apple, but I'm still starving."

"I'll be ready in five. I promise. Then we can go fill your tummy, so you can stop whining."

"I'm not whining."

"You are." I smiled as I pulled my hair back into a ponytail.

We climbed into the back of the limo, stopped at a diner for breakfast, then headed to Long Island. I had no clue what it was he wanted to show me, but I sure as hell was curious to find out.

"Feel better now that your tummy is nice and full?" I smirked.

"Actually, I do. You seemed to fully enjoy those Belgian waffles you ordered."

"I did."

"More than my cock?" A cunning smile crossed his lips.

"Let's just say both satisfy me in different ways."

We were on a dirt winding road for about a half a mile before passing through a double white gate that led to a two-story red brick sprawling mansion with trees that lined the surrounding area for maximum privacy.

"What is this place?" I asked as Wyatt helped me from the limo.

"This is my home away from the city." He smiled.

I stood there, looking around, and took in the peacefulness of the area as a light wind swept across my face.

"This is where I come to get away from it all. My mother loved it here."

A smile crossed my lips as I hooked my arm around his and he led me around the house, towards the back where four horses were out grazing.

"Mr. Coleman. I didn't expect to see you today." An older woman smiled as she walked up to us.

"Hello, Betsy. It was kind of a last-minute decision. I'd like you to meet Laurel Holloway. Laurel, this is Betsy. She and her husband Jerry take care of the place for me."

"It's nice to meet you, Laurel."

"You as well, Betsy," I spoke as I placed my hand in hers.

"There's someone else I'd like you to meet," Wyatt spoke as he led me to where the horses were grazing. "Hey, buddy. How are you today?" He smiled as he ran his hand across his back. "This is my horse, Apollo. Apollo, I'd like you to meet Laurel."

"Hello there." I smiled as I ran my hand down his mane. "He's beautiful. Well, well, Mr. Coleman, I would have never

The Interview: New York & Los Angeles

in a million years taken you for a horse guy."

"My grandfather owned this place. My mom, sister, and I spent a lot of summers here growing up. When he passed away, he left it to us. So, I've been around horses my whole life."

"Your mother never remarried?" I asked.

"Nah. She dated a few men, but with her having MS, she didn't want to have to put anyone through that, so nothing ever got serious. Do you like horses?"

"I do." I grinned. "He's an Arabian, right?"

"Yes. Have you ever ridden?"

"I have. Several times," I replied.

"Good. Because today, we're going to ride." He smiled.

"Whose white horse is that?" I pointed.

"That's Arabella, Sammi's horse. Isn't she a beauty?"

"She certainly is." I smiled.

"And the black horse next to Arabella is Callie. You'll be riding her."

"She's beautiful as well."

"Hey, Betsy?" Wyatt called out. "Can you take Apollo and Callie and get them ready to ride?"

"Of course, Mr. Coleman."

As soon as the horses were ready, Wyatt helped me up onto Callie and then hopped onto Apollo, and we set off to some trails not too far from the house.

"It's so beautiful out here, Wyatt."

"I know. Like I said earlier, this is where I come to get away from it all."

"How often do you come out here?"

"As often as I can. I usually come out here on Sundays for the day. Sometimes, I'll escape for the weekend, depending on if Sammi and her boyfriend are here or not."

"Do you escape alone, or do you like to bring someone with you?" I arched my brow as I glanced over at him.

"Alone. I don't ever bring anyone here."

"And yet you brought me?"

"I figured it would be good for the article. Just don't put the location of this place."

"I won't." I smiled. "But I will need to get some pictures of you on that horse. We can do it out here."

We rode for a while longer and then I climbed off Callie and took some pictures of Wyatt on his horse. My heart skipped several beats as I clicked each picture. Suddenly, my phone dinged with a text message from Eric.

"I booked a flight back to Seattle for you. Your plane takes off tomorrow at noon. I need you back here, Laurel. No attitude. I'll send George to pick you up from the airport."

A sick feeling erupted in the pit of my stomach and I didn't respond.

"Are you okay?" Wyatt asked.

"Yeah." I forced a smile. "I just got a text message from my boss, Eric. He booked me a flight back to Seattle tomorrow at noon. He needs me back in the office."

"I see. Well then, we better make the most of the time we have left. Let's head back to the ranch. Betsy is making dinner for us and then we'll head back to the city."

The Interview: New York & Los Angeles

"Sounds good," I spoke as I climbed back on Callie and we turned around and headed back.

Chapter Twenty-Eight

We got back to the city, and as soon as we stepped into his penthouse, Wyatt grabbed my hand and led me upstairs to the bathroom, where he started the shower.

"You're taking a shower?" I asked.

"No. We're taking a shower together." He winked at me as he grabbed two towels from the cabinet.

I walked over to the oversized tub and started the water.

"What are you doing?" Wyatt asked.

"I'd rather take a bath."

"Seriously, Laurel?"

"Yes. I happen to love relaxing baths. Do you have any bubbles?"

"No. Why would I have bubbles?"

"Oh wait. I took some from the hotel." I grinned.

"We're not taking a bath. We're taking a shower," he shouted as I walked out of the bathroom.

I opened my suitcase and grabbed the small bottle of bubble bath I stole from the Four Seasons Hotel in California.

"Then by all means, Mr. Coleman, take your shower."

The Interview: New York & Los Angeles

I sat on the edge of the tub, squeezed some of the bubble bath under the running stream of water, and heard him turn the shower off. Looking back, I spoke, "Changed your mind?"

He took in a sharp breath as he shook his finger at me.

"Oh come on. It's okay to admit that you like bubble baths."

"I've never taken a bubble bath in my life, Miss Holloway."

"Never? I can honestly tell you that you're missing out on one of the pleasures in life."

"Somehow I doubt that," he spoke as he stripped out of his clothes.

He climbed in first. I removed my clothes and followed him in, snuggling in between his legs and resting my back against his chest. He wrapped his arms around me and I slowly closed my eyes, trying not to think about how this was going to be the last night I'd be with him.

"Are you okay?" he asked as his fingers softly stroked my arm.

"Of course. Why do you ask?" I tilted my head back and looked up at him.

"You suddenly got quiet."

"I'm fine. I'm just dreading all the work I have to do when I get back to Seattle. Not to mention Eric biting my head off when he gets the credit card bill."

"I'm pretty sure you can handle Eric." He smiled. "Listen, I have to be in the office early tomorrow morning for an important meeting, so I'll have Ryan drive you to the airport."

"Yeah. Okay. Sure."

"Turn around," he spoke.

I did as he asked, and he brought his hand up to my cheek and softly stroked it before brushing his lips against mine.

"I guess your interview is complete."

"I guess so." I kissed him.

"I want to fuck you right here, right now in this tub, but I don't have any condoms close by."

"I'm on birth control if it makes you feel better. I have been for years." The corners of my mouth curved upwards.

"Then by all means, climb aboard." He grinned.

Elation soared through me as my body orgasmed at the same time as Wyatt. Our lips tangled with passion as a deep moan erupted from him.

"What do you think about bubble baths now?" I smirked.

"I absolutely love them."

We climbed out of the tub and Wyatt wrapped a towel around me before drying himself off. It might not have seemed like anything big to others, but to me, it made my heart melt. After drying off, we climbed into bed and I laid my head against his chest while his arms held me in place.

"I wish I could take you to the airport tomorrow," he spoke.

"It's not a big deal. I know you have an important meeting. Plus, I'm a big girl. I travel to and from airports alone all the time."

We both fell asleep, and when I awoke the next morning, I found him in the kitchen all dressed and ready to head to the office.

"Why didn't you wake me?" I asked.

"I was going to in a minute right before I left." He looked at

The Interview: New York & Los Angeles

his watch. "I actually have to leave now or else I'll be late. He walked over to where I stood and wrapped his arms around my waist.

"If you're ever in New York again, call me." His lips formed a smile.

Say what? Really?

"Yeah. I will. Thanks for the interview."

"You're welcome and thank you for keeping me company the past few days. I enjoyed getting to know you, Laurel Holloway." He kissed my lips.

Here I was on the brink of devastation that I had to leave him and say goodbye and he acted like it was no big deal.

"The pleasure was all mine, Mr. Coleman."

His lips brushed against mine one last time before he picked up his briefcase and headed towards the elevator.

"Call Ryan when you're ready to leave. Have a safe flight."

"Thanks. Hey," I spoke and he turned around. "Keep in touch."

The corners of his mouth curved up into a smile. "I will."

He stepped onto the elevator, and when the door shut, I stood there staring at them, hoping and praying they'd open back up and he'd come running out and swoop me up in his arms. But they didn't, and as hard as I tried to hold back the tears, they forcefully streamed down my face.

"You stupid stupid girl. You knew what the fucking consequences would be if you fell for him, but you did it anyway." I scolded myself. *"You knew from day one what type of man he was. What made you think you were any different? Because he invited you to stay at his home? Because you were the only woman he took to his ranch? You know the rules,*

Laurel, and you broke them. You let every emotion buried inside you emerge and look what happened. For fuck sakes, he thanked you for your company like you were a goddamn prostitute. Except he didn't pay you in cash; he gave you the interview you wanted."

My job here in New York was done, and I needed to leave right now. I couldn't wait four more hours before my flight left, so I called the airport to see if I could get on another flight. Luckily, there was one flight leaving in an hour and a half out of LaGuardia. I didn't have time to call Ryan, so I grabbed my bags and had the doorman hail me a cab.

"Where to, lady?"

"LaGuardia Airport."

As I was sitting in the back of the cab, I just needed to hear Wyatt's voice one last time. God, what the hell was wrong with me? I knew he was in a meeting, so I called his office phone.

"Good morning, Mr. Coleman's office, this is Tamara, how can I help you?"

"Tamara, it's Laurel."

"Hi, Laurel. What can I do for you?"

"I know Wyatt is in a meeting, but could you leave a message for him to call me when he gets out?"

"Mr. Coleman isn't in a meeting this morning. He's in his office. I can put you through."

"NO. Don't. Did his meeting get cancelled?"

"He never had a meeting scheduled for today. Are you okay?"

That same sick feeling in the pit of my belly emerged again.

"I'm fine. Listen, Tamara, please don't tell him I called.

The Interview: New York & Los Angeles

Okay? I'm actually begging you."

"I won't say a word, Laurel. I promise. Are you still in New York?"

"I'm on my way to the airport to go back to Seattle."

"I see. Whatever he did, I'm so sorry. You don't deserve it."

"Thanks. But it's not what he did, it's what he didn't do. Have a good day, Tamara, and thank you."

"You're welcome. Have a safe flight back home. Hopefully, I'll see you again."

I ended the call and took in a deep breath. He lied to me. He never had a meeting. He just didn't want to feel obligated to take me to the airport. My sadness subsided, and anger took its place.

"Can you please step on it? I need to get out of this fucking state!" I snapped at the cab driver.

"Calm down, lady. There's traffic. I'm doing the best I can."

"Do better. You New York cab drivers are notorious for almost killing your passengers with your erratic driving."

He glared at me through the rearview mirror and didn't say a word.

Chapter Twenty-Nine

I'd finally landed in Seattle, and before the plane took off from New York, I sent a text message to George telling him of my flight change and asked him to pick me up. If there was anyone I needed the most right now, it was my best friend.

The moment I saw him standing in the baggage pickup area, I stopped and stared at him. He tilted his head with a sympathetic look and I lost it. I ran into his arms and sobbed like a crazy fool in front of everyone in the area.

"Shh. It's okay, Laurel." He held me tight. "Everything's going to be okay."

"He told me that if I was ever in New York again to call him," I cried.

"He's an asshole, sweetheart. Come on, we have to get your bags and then we'll get out of here and talk."

I stood there next to him with my head on his shoulder while we waited for my bags to come around. Suddenly, my phone dinged with a text message from Wyatt and my heart started racing.

"Ryan said you never called him to take you to the airport? What's going on?"

"Don't respond, Laurel," George spoke. "Just don't. You have to cut all ties with him now."

The Interview: New York & Los Angeles

My bags finally came around and I shoved my phone into my purse. George drove me home, and the second I stepped inside, I collapsed on the couch.

"You are Laurel Holloway and you're going to be okay," George spoke as he grabbed my hand.

"I don't know about this time. I fell in love with his dumb ass." Tears streamed down my face again. "I don't fall in love. But with him, it just happened. I lost all control, George, and I hate myself."

"Laurel, stop. You're human. That's why you fell for him. This wall you've spent building all these years was bound to come crumbling down one of these days. You're not a robot, darling. You have the same emotions as everyone else in the world."

"I hate him."

"No, you don't. You love him, and he broke your heart. You hate what he did to you, not him."

"I'm going to go take a bath. On second thought, no, I'm not. I don't think I can ever take a bath again."

George let out a light chuckle.

"Do you remember what you told me when Kairi broke up with me?"

"Never let anyone have that kind of power over your emotional state," I softly spoke.

"That's right." He ran his hand down my hair. "How about me and Veronica come over tonight and we'll binge watch movies and eat a bunch of junk food?"

"As tempting as that sounds, I really just want to be alone."

He pulled his phone from his pocket when he heard a text message come through.

"Eric needs me back in the office. Are you sure about tonight?"

"I'm sure. Thanks." I managed a half smile.

He kissed my forehead and walked out the door. I changed into a pair of sweatpants and a tank top and climbed into bed with my phone. I knew I shouldn't have done it, but I did. I replied back to Wyatt.

"I decided to take an earlier flight out and there wasn't time to call Ryan."

I shut my phone off and took a nap.

****

I awoke to the ringing sound of my doorbell. Stumbling out of bed, I looked through the peephole and saw it was Eric. Sighing, I opened the door.

"Welcome home, Laurel."

"Eric, this isn't a good time."

"I know it's not and you look like shit. I brought us dinner and we're going to talk."

He pushed his way past me and went into the kitchen.

"What time is it?"

"Seven o'clock. I tried calling you, but it went straight to voicemail."

"That's because I have my phone turned off."

"Avoiding calls or text messages from certain people?" he asked as he took the cartons of Thai food from the plastic bag. "I warned you about falling for him."

"Eric, what are you doing here?"

The Interview: New York & Los Angeles

"George told me what happened and not of his own free will either, so you can't be mad at him. I came to check up on you, kid."

"Thanks." My voice softened. "But I'm fine."

I took down a couple of plates from the cabinet and a bottle of wine from the wine rack.

"No, you're not. Where's my perky little Laurel who doesn't take bullshit from anyone?"

"She got hurt, Eric," I spoke as I took a seat at the table.

"But the Laurel I know won't let that hurt keep her down for too long. She's resilient and strong. You're one of the strongest women I know."

"Maybe I'm not so strong after all. I let myself fall for him when I knew the risk. He prefers a garden of flowers versus a single one."

"What? What kind of nonsense is that?"

"There was a part of me for a moment that thought maybe I could be the exceptional flower. The rare one that would drown out all the others. God, I'm such an idiot."

"Laurel, you're not an idiot. There's obviously a mutual attraction between the both of you. Plus, long distance relationships never work. Especially with a man like that. You'd always be wondering what the hell he was doing. You already have massive trust issues as it is."

"I suppose you're right. Even if he did see me as something more, it never would have worked. Plus, we're both so busy with our careers."

"Exactly. Chalk this experience up to nothing more than a good time. You had fun with him. Let it be that and get on with your life. Bigger and better things are waiting for you, kid. You're young and you have your whole life ahead of you still."

"Thanks, Eric." I managed a smile.

"That's what I'm here for. Not only as your boss but as your life coach."

"Let's not push it." I pointed at him.

"Have you even started the article yet?" he asked.

"No. I'm going to need a couple of days to do that."

"Take whatever time you need. I got a call today and the powers that be put a hold on the magazine publication for next month."

"Why?"

"Not sure. All they said was that there's a problem they need to work out."

"What about Everything Laurel?"

"Well, we're still going to publish that online and in the paper. It hasn't officially moved to the magazine yet."

Eric and I talked for a while longer and then he left. Even though I gave him shit all the time, he was a good friend. I cleaned up the kitchen and went to my bedroom and turned on my phone. My heart started rapidly beating as I waited for it to load with the hopes there would be a text message or voicemail from Wyatt. There wasn't, so I climbed into bed and somehow managed to fall asleep.

A couple of weeks had passed, and it was still a struggle to erase him from my mind. I found myself merely existing and everyone around me knew it. I kept myself busy with Everything Laurel and a few other articles I voluntarily took on. Craig and I talked just about every day. He was the one good thing that came out of doing the interviews.

"Hey you." George smiled as he stepped into my office. "One Grande Americano with a double shot of espresso," he

The Interview: New York & Los Angeles

spoke as he held up the Starbucks cup.

"Thanks." I sighed. "I'm thinking about going to Boston this weekend."

"Why?" His brows furrowed. "I figured with the state you're in right now, that's the last place you'd want to be."

"Right? My parents are throwing Alfie and Celia an engagement party and requested my presence." I rolled my eyes.

"Wait a minute. Didn't you tell me he was shacking up on the couch at your Airbnb in New York with some other chick?"

"Yep." I sighed. "I really don't want to go and celebrate something that isn't going to last, but it'll get my mind off you know who. You know the shenanigans that always happen at a Holloway party. Oh, I have an idea, come with me."

"I would in a heartbeat, but me and Veronica are going to Lake Tahoe this weekend."

My phone rang. It was Bella calling.

"Grab that; we'll talk later." George smiled as he walked out of my office.

"Hey, Bella," I answered.

"Hey, sis. Did you book your flight yet?"

"No. I was just going to. Why?"

"Fly to New York Thursday night, stay with me, and then we can drive together Friday. It'll be fun since we didn't get to spend any time together at all when you were here."

"What about Thaddeus?"

"He can't go to the party and he's leaving Thursday for a business trip. He won't be back until Sunday night. Please. It'll just be us sisters." She whined.

"Okay. I'll see what flights are available."

"Oh my God! I'm so happy. We're going to have so much fun! Text me your flight information and I'll pick you up from the airport."

"Thanks, Bella, but I'll just take a cab to your apartment. There's no need for you to drive all the way to the airport."

"Are you sure? I don't mind."

"I'm positive. I'll see you Thursday night."

I pulled up the flights to New York and there was only one that was a possibility.

"Hey, Eric, do you have a second?" I asked as I walked into his office.

"I always have a second for you, Laurel." He smiled.

"Is it okay if I take both Thursday and Friday off?"

"Why Thursday?"

"My sister wants me to fly into New York and then drive with her to Boston Friday morning."

"That's fine. You have plenty of vacation time. Do you really think going back to New York is such a good idea right now?"

"It's not like I'm going to see him or anything."

"I know, but—"

"But?" I narrowed my eye at him.

"Nothing. Take the two days and have fun with your family. It'll do you some good."

The Interview: New York & Los Angeles

"Fun with my family never does me any good, Eric." I smiled.

"This time it will." He winked.

"Thanks. I owe you." I pointed at him before walking out of his office.

Chapter Thirty

My plane landed in New York at approximately eight eleven pm and by time I got to Bella's apartment, it was almost nine o'clock.

"Eeek," she screeched when she opened the door. "I'm so happy you're here."

"It's good to see you, Bella." I gave her a hug.

Even though we weren't as close as two sisters should be, somehow, I felt better seeing her. We put on our pajamas, made some popcorn, drank some wine, and talked.

"I'm really glad you're here." Her eyes swelled with tears.

"Bella, what's wrong?"

"Thaddeus didn't go on a business trip. We broke up and he moved out."

"Aw, sweetie. I'm sorry. What happened?"

"I just wasn't happy. I haven't told Mom and Dad yet, so please don't say anything."

I reached over and took hold of her hands.

"I won't say anything. If you weren't happy, you did the right thing by breaking it off."

The Interview: New York & Los Angeles

"Mom and Dad are going to be pissed. They loved him."

"Who cares. Your life isn't their life. You have to do what's best for you, not them."

"I know." She sniffled as she wiped the tear from her cheek. "I always admired you, Laurel. You are so strong and don't give a damn what anyone thinks, especially our parents. I really look up to you."

"That's sweet, little sister, but I'm not as strong as you think I am." My eyes filled with tears.

I told her about Wyatt, and the both of us sat and cried together. For the first time, I felt connected to my sister.

The next morning, we hopped into Bella's car and decided to stop and grab some breakfast first since we had a four-hour drive back to our childhood home.

"Have you ever eaten at Sarabeth's?" Bella asked.

"No. Is the food good?"

"Oh my God! It's on the Upper East Side and they have the most amazing coconut pancakes."

"Sounds delicious. I love coconut and pancakes." I grinned.

She parallel parked along the curb and we walked a few feet down the sidewalk until we reached Sarabeth's. I stopped dead in my tracks as we passed the window and I saw Wyatt sitting at a table with another woman.

"Laurel, what's wrong?" she asked.

I placed my hand over my rapidly pounding heart and a sickness fell inside me.

"Wyatt's here."

"Shit. We'll go somewhere else." She grabbed my hand and

started pulling me along.

"No. We're going to eat here. I want coconut pancakes and I'm having them. I'm not letting Mr. Wyatt Coleman keep me from that. I'll just pretend I don't see him."

"Are you sure? I think it's best we go somewhere else."

"I'm positive."

I took in a long deep breath before entering the restaurant and kept my eyes away from him. The band aid that was over my heart while it was trying to heal was torn off and the wound reopened, leaving me in more pain than before. Seeing him with that redhead who looked to be at least ten years older than him made my blood boil. The hostess started to seat us in a booth that was across from them.

"Excuse me. No. No. No. We cannot sit there. Perhaps you have a table over on this side." I pointed.

"I'm sorry, but I can't seat you in that section."

"Why not? There are plenty of tables available."

"But there's only one waitress on that side and she already has more tables than she should."

"Listen," I looked at her name tag on her uniform, "Courtney, for reasons I can't explain, I cannot sit at that booth. In fact, I need to be as far away from that table where the hot and sexy man and the redhead are sitting. Got it?" I arched my brow.

"Oh. I think I do. Are you his mistress and that's his wife?" she asked with a whisper.

"Yeah. Sure. That's it. So please seat us somewhere else."

"Okay. I understand."

As soon as Bella and I placed our order, I needed to use the

The Interview: New York & Los Angeles

restroom.

"Do you know where the restrooms are?" I asked her. "And please don't tell me they're on the other side of the restaurant? Because if they are, I can hold it."

She let out a light laugh. "They're down that hallway right there. The first door on the left is the women's."

"I'll be right back."

After I washed my hands, I dried them off, and when I opened the door to step out, Wyatt nearly knocked me over.

"I'm sor—" He looked at me in shock. "Laurel? What are you doing here?"

Fuck. Fuck. Fuck. My knees began to shake as his scent infiltrated the small narrow space.

"Wyatt?" I looked at my watch. "Shouldn't you be at the office?" I asked, as I needed to play it cool.

"I'm here meeting someone for breakfast," he replied and the sickness inside me grew. "You didn't answer my question. What are you doing back in New York?"

Frankly, it was none of his damn business why I was here. I didn't owe him shit. Especially an explanation. He was nothing to me but a man I interviewed for a magazine article.

"I'm here with my sister. It was good to see you, Wyatt." I tried to walk past him, but he wouldn't move out of the way. Damn these small New York restaurants.

"Didn't I tell you to call me if you were ever back in New York?" he spoke sternly.

"That's right, you did." I smiled. "To be honest, I'd forgotten and me and my sister have plans. But, like I said, it was good to see you." I squeezed my way past him and went back to the table, where I could barely breathe.

"You didn't take your phone with you. I tried to warn you he was on his way to the bathroom. Are you okay?"

"I'm fine." I took a sip of my coffee.

"No, you're not, sis."

"I am. I think I needed to see him one last time because the conversation we just had made me feel so much better."

She sat across from me with a narrowed eye, disbelieving everything I said. The waitress came over and set our plates of coconut pancakes down in front of us. I glanced over at the hallway and saw him emerge from the bathroom. Instantly, I looked away but could see him coming towards our table from the corner of my eye.

"Shit," I spoke.

"Laurel, I need to speak to you for a moment," he spoke.

"Wyatt, this is my sister, Bella. Bella, this is Wyatt Coleman. He's the man I interviewed while I was here a couple of weeks ago."

"Nice to meet you, Wyatt."

"Nice to meet you as well, Bella. I was at your ballet performance. You were very good."

"Thank you." She grinned in a flirtatious way, and I lightly kicked her under the table.

"Seriously, Laurel, I need to speak to you."

"I'm sorry, Wyatt, but now isn't a good time. Bella and I are on a time restriction and we need to hurry up and eat."

"Yeah. We need to get on the road to Boston. Our parents are throwing our brother an engagement party," Bella spoke.

Once again, I kicked her under the table for spilling all that

The Interview: New York & Los Angeles

information to him.

"I see. Well then, I guess our conversation can wait for another time," he spoke. "It was really good to see you, Laurel."

"It was, wasn't it?" I put on a happy face. "Enjoy your breakfast, Wyatt. It's very rude to keep your company waiting."

"Have a safe drive to Boston," he spoke as he glared at me before walking away.

"Oh my God! That was spectacular!" Bella exclaimed. "You handled that so well, sis. I'm so proud of you."

I gave her a smile and ate my pancakes. I was still hurting inside. Hurting like a bitch to be exact. But, like I told Bella, I think I needed to see him again, because now, I could put closure on everything. What exactly was I putting closure on? I was putting closure on the fact that I fell in love with him and he didn't love me back.

Sandi Lynn

Chapter Thirty-One

My parents had really outdone themselves on this one. It looked like a freaking wedding was going to take place instead of an engagement party. White tents lined the backyard with lights that could be seen a mile away. Tables draped in white and pink filled the spaces and were elegantly decorated with floral arrangements of white lilies and pink roses. Fine white china, crystal glasses, and sterling silver silverware occupied eight spaces around the tables. A special spot was designated for the D.J. as he set up and the bartenders were already in place. The pool was filled with pink rose petals and a couple of swans who eloquently glided among them. The waiters wore black pants and silk black shirts while the waitresses wore short black dresses with white aprons tied around their waists. The caterers scurried around the kitchen, prepping food, making sure everything was ready when the guests arrived. The occasion was formal, so I wore the dress I wore to Wyatt's fundraiser.

"That's a nice dress, Laurel," my mother spoke as she looked me up and down. "Who's the designer?"

"No one you would know. I got it at Nordstrom, right off the mannequin, and it only cost a hundred bucks." I smiled, for I knew that would irritate her.

She took in a sharp breath and inhaled the tequila she was holding in her hand.

"You really went all out for this engagement party," I spoke as I sipped my wine.

"You could have this too if you had a man in your life." Her brow arched.

And here we go.

"And get cheated on? No thanks."

Okay, I'd admit that was a low blow, but I was sick and tired of her hounding me about not being in a relationship. She didn't know the pain I was going through at the moment.

"If you're making some type of accusation against your brother, you're wrong. Alfie loves Celia very much."

"Keep telling yourself that, Mom," I spoke as I walked away and took a seat on the outdoor swing next to Bella. "When are you going to tell Mom and Dad about you and Thaddeus?"

"Tomorrow. I don't want to upset them. This party means a lot."

"Well, let me know when you decide to do it because I'll be there to have your back." I smiled as I hooked my arm around her and Alfie snapped a picture.

"Ah, sisterly love," he spoke.

"I need to talk to you since you weren't around last night," I spoke as I got up from the swing, hooked my arm around his, and led him to the gazebo.

"What about?"

"I'm hoping your little affairs are over."

"Yeah, sure." He tried to sound convincing.

"Listen, Alfie, Celia loves you to the moon and back. I see the light in her eyes every time she looks at you. If you can't keep your dick in your pants, then break it off. I don't want to see her get hurt."

"Chill out, Laurel. I've got things under control."

"Let me ask you this. What if she was sleeping around with other men?"

"I'd fucking kill her and the guy."

"Then why is it okay for you to do it?"

"I didn't say it was okay. Sometimes I need something different. Celia doesn't exactly fulfill me in the sexual department."

"Then why the fuck are you marrying her?!" I shouted.

"Because we're good together in every other way. Men have special needs, sis. There are things I want that Celia won't do. So, if I get it from somewhere else, then that means I'm happy, and if I'm happy, Celia is happy."

"Oh my God! You certainly have your father's blood running through you. Ugh! Karma's a bitch, little brother. I've already warned you about that."

"I don't believe in karma. Stop worrying about me and Celia and worry about your own love life," he scowled as he walked away.

I needed something stronger than wine. The guests started to pour in and the music started to play. I went up to the bar and asked the bartender for a neat martini straight up with two olives. As I was standing there with my elbows rested against the counter, I heard my father's voice from behind.

"Laurel, sweetheart, look who's here."

I turned around and froze when I saw Wyatt standing next to my father.

"Hello, Laurel. It's good to see you again."

The Interview: New York & Los Angeles

I swallowed hard.

"Hello, Wyatt. What are you doing here?" My lips gave way to a fake smile, so my father wouldn't suspect anything.

"Your father invited me. I wasn't sure until the last minute if I was going to be able to make it or not."

"I'll let the two of you talk," my father spoke. "I have to go greet some of the other guests."

I needed to play this smooth. There was no way I could let on to the fact that he broke my heart and that I had been a psychotic mess ever since I left New York.

"What's going on, Laurel?" he asked.

I grabbed my martini from the bar and downed it.

"Another one, please," I spoke to the bartender. "What do you mean?"

"You were very cold to me at the restaurant yesterday."

"I apologize if I was. I didn't mean to be. Why didn't you tell me you were coming tonight?"

"Why didn't you tell me you were in New York?" His eye narrowed.

"I asked first," I spoke as I arched my brow.

"You're not winning this one, darling. I'll answer your question as soon as you answer mine."

"Then I guess you're never getting your answer." I smirked.

"Wyatt Coleman." An older man approached us. "How are you, son?"

"I'm excellent, Joe. Give me just a second."

As I started to walk away, Wyatt lightly took hold of my arm and whispered in my ear.

"I will get an answer, even if I have to fuck it out of you."

I swallowed hard as the hair on my arms stood tall.

"Never going to happen. We had our fun and now I'm having fun with someone else."

I walked away with my drink in my hand.

The Interview: New York & Los Angeles

Chapter Thirty-Two

Dinner was being served and everyone was asked to please take their seats. At the back of the tent was a small rectangular table for two where Celia and Alfie sat as though they were on display for everyone to admire. I took a seat at our family table next to Bella.

"What the fuck is going on? Why is Wyatt here?" she asked.

"Apparently, Dad invited him."

"Why?"

"I don't know. He won't tell me until I tell him why I didn't tell him I was in New York."

"Then ask Dad."

"I couldn't find him."

I looked up and saw my mother walking towards the table with Wyatt on her arm.

"You may sit with us, Wyatt," she spoke. "In fact, sit next to Laurel since the two of you already know each other." She smiled.

One. Two. Three. Calm down.

"I'm surprised you showed up." He leaned closer and whispered in my ear.

"I really didn't have a choice."

"Who is this person you're having fun with?"

"A guy I met when I got back to Seattle," I lied.

"Then all I can say is he has excellent taste in women."

"Damn right he does."

I heard Bella snicker, so I lightly kicked her under the table.

"Bella, baby, I'm so sad Thaddeus couldn't make it. Who knows, maybe we'll be doing this again soon. God knows you're our last hope." My mother glanced at me.

I took in a long deep breath as I felt Wyatt's hand gently squeeze my thigh under the table.

"Stay calm, Laurel. Ignore her," he whispered.

My father finally joined us, and I noticed one of his buttons on his shirt was undone. That explained why I couldn't find him. This was too much, and I was going to snap. My mother and her snide comments, Alfie's piss poor attitude and lack of respect towards Celia, my father having sex with someone other than my mother at his son's engagement party, and Wyatt Coleman, the man whore himself showing up and sitting next to me. This was a bad idea coming here.

"Adalynn, why is your tennis coach here?" my father asked.

"Why not? He's known Alfie for a long time. Maybe I can ask the same about your secretary."

"That's the tennis coach?" Wyatt whispered as he nodded to the next table.

"Yep. Sitting right next to the secretary."

Dinner was over, and cake was being served when Alfie stood up and demanded everyone's attention, so he could give

The Interview: New York & Los Angeles

a gushing speech about his future wife. As he was in the middle of telling everyone that Celia was his soulmate, a woman walked in and interrupted. All eyes turned to her.

"Alfie, I didn't know any other way to get your attention. You won't return my text messages or my phone calls."

"Charlotte, what are you doing here?"

"Alfie, who's that?" Celia asked with a nervousness in her voice.

"Who is that?" Wyatt asked me.

"I'm going to say it's one of the women he's been sleeping with."

Shit was about to get real for the Holloway family and I was just going to sit back and watch it all go down.

"She's a friend," Alfie replied. "I have no idea what she's talking about, but I'll take care of it."

"A friend? Is that all I am to you? That's not what you told me the last time we were together."

"Charlotte, I don't know what you're talking about. Dad, can you please have her escorted out?"

"I'm fucking pregnant, you idiot!" she screamed from across the tent.

My brow raised, my mother placed her hand over her chest, and my father sat there shaking his head.

"Welcome to my dysfunctional family." I glanced over at Wyatt.

"Yes, indeed. I can see now what you were talking about."

Discussions got heated. Celia stood there in full blown shock as tears streamed down her face. Her mother and father ran to her side. My mother stood up and chimed in and let the poor girl have it.

"I don't know who the hell you think you are, but you are to leave the premises immediately! Alfie is engaged to be married and you come to my home with this preposterous story! Only a trashy woman would do such a thing. It's obvious you have no idea whom you're dealing with."

"I'm pregnant and your son is the father!" she shouted. "He told me I was special and that he was going to break up with her." She pointed to Celia.

"My son would never cheat on his fiancée," she growled. "You're delusional and if it's money you want, you can forget it."

A man whom my father hired to keep an eye on things, came and grabbed her by the arm and tried to escort her out, but she wasn't going without a fight. I stood up, walked over, and smacked the hand around her arm.

"Let go of her! She's pregnant, for God sakes."

"Laurel Marie Holloway, come sit down now!" my mother demanded.

"No. I'm not going to sit down, Mother. This woman came here because your perfect little son wouldn't return her calls. Out of desperation, she came here to protect what was hers the only way she knew how."

"Laurel, that's enough!" my father shouted as he stood up.

"Sit down and shut up, Dad! I'm sorry, everyone, but the party has come to an end. There's nothing more to see here. So please gather your things and leave. My family thanks you for coming."

The guests started to scurry out of the tent as my mother and father stood there in shock. I walked back over to the table as

The Interview: New York & Los Angeles

the moment of truth had come.

"For years, I've stood by as an outsider while the two of you painted your real children out to be these perfect specimens you created. For years, I took criticism from you while you gave them nothing but praise. You think your son couldn't be a cheater? Think again, Mother. He gets it from his parents. The two people who were supposed to be role models."

"Laurel, how dare you!" my mother shouted with disgust.

"Shut up, Mother! I'm sick to death of all the lies and secrets with this family. Why the hell do you think I moved three thousand miles away and never come home? Dad, Mom knows you're sleeping around with any woman who looks your way. She's known for years. And guess what? She's sleeping with the pool boy and her tennis coach. Poor Bella over here broke up with Thaddeus because she was so unhappy but afraid to tell you. And Alfie over here," I pointed, "he's no saint. He takes after you, Dad, and hell, who can blame him? It's what he was taught."

"It's no wonder why no one wants you," my mother lashed out. "You are nothing but a liar and a horrible human being."

I held out my arms. "That's where you're wrong, Mom. I'm the most normal one in this place because I don't have your fucking blood running through my veins. I'm the real deal and you can't handle it. My whole life I was treated as if I didn't belong in this family. Nothing I did was ever good enough, and when something went wrong, I was always to blame, even when it wasn't my fault. YOU reminded me time and time again that I wasn't your real child! As soon as Alfie and Bella were born, I was pushed to the side, and whatever I wanted to do didn't matter."

"Laurel, please stop," Bella cried.

"You want to know why I don't have a boyfriend, because it's my choice. MINE! How the hell am I supposed to trust anyone? And for the record, I didn't break up with David because we grew apart. I broke up with him because when I went back to college after Bella's birthday party, I walked in on him and my best friend."

"You never told me that," my mother spoke.

"No. And you want to know why? Because in your eyes, it somehow would have been my fault that he cheated on me."

"Laurel, I had no idea you felt this way," my father spoke.

"How could you? Seriously, how could any of you? You were too busy with your other children and your affairs to even notice anything I was going through."

"You have disgraced this family and I think it's best that you leave this house," my mother spoke.

"Dad?" I stared at him.

"Your mother is right."

"Nothing would give me more pleasure." I narrowed my eye and shook my head. I turned to Alfie. "Still don't believe in karma? I warned you, little brother," I spoke as I stormed off.

"Laurel, no!" Bella cried.

The Interview: New York & Los Angeles

Chapter Thirty-Three

"Laurel, wait!" Wyatt yelled as he ran after me.

"Leave me alone, Wyatt. I can't deal with you right now."

I ran up to my room, grabbed my suitcase, and started throwing my stuff in it.

"What the hell did I do that's making you have this attitude towards me?"

"You know what?" I stopped and faced him. "The reason I didn't tell you I was in New York was because you couldn't even be bothered to call or text me after I left. And you lied about having a meeting that morning." Tears filled my eyes. "I called Tamara to have her give you a message and she told me you never had a meeting scheduled."

"I can explain why I lied."

"I don't want to hear your excuses. I waited for you to call me or even just send a text to say hi. But you didn't, and you know what? I'm the fool for letting my guard down when I knew better."

"You don't understand, Laurel!" he shouted.

"Oh, I clearly understand, Wyatt," I spoke as I shut my suitcase and headed down the stairs.

Once I reached the front door, I placed my hand on the

doorknob, stopped, and looked at him.

"What I understand is that my absence didn't affect you, so clearly my presence never mattered." I opened the door, walked out, and had my father's driver take me to the airport.

****

"How may I help you?" the attendant behind the ticket counter asked.

"I need to get on your next flight to Seattle."

"Okay. Let me check to see when our next flight leaves. Unfortunately, the next flight out isn't until six a.m. tomorrow morning."

"Shit. Okay. How about a flight to Los Angeles?"

She began clicking the keys on her keyboard and then lightly shook her head.

"Same. I'm sorry."

"Damn it. Okay, how about a flight to New York City and then from there a flight to Los Angeles?"

"We have a flight that leaves for New York in about thirty minutes, and from there you can catch the next flight to Los Angeles, but you're only going to have about ten minutes to catch that plane before it takes off."

"I'll take it."

"Are you sure? If your incoming plane is late, you won't make the next flight."

"It's the chance I'm going to have to take. I need to get out of Boston tonight."

As soon as she handed me my tickets, I flew through security, thanking God for the short line, and I ran to my gate. I

The Interview: New York & Los Angeles

made it, took my seat, and then let out a deep breath. Pulling out my phone, I called Craig.

"Hey, Laurel. What's up?" he answered as I could hear a lot of background noise coming from his kitchen.

"Are you working late tonight?"

"Yeah. I'll be leaving here around midnight. Why?"

"I'm flying into Los Angeles and my plane gets in around twelve forty a.m."

"Are you okay?"

"No. Actually, I'm not. I'm a hot mess right now and I don't want to go home."

"Where are you?"

"I'm in Boston right now, just about to take off to New York, and then I'm flying into L.A. from there. I'll explain everything."

"I'll pick you up from the airport and you can stay at my place."

"I don't want to interrupt your plans with Maddy."

"Maddy is out of town this weekend visiting her parents. She won't be back until late tomorrow night."

"Okay. Thanks, Craig."

"You're welcome, sweetheart. I'll see you later. Have a safe flight."

"Excuse me, miss? You need to turn off your phone now. We're about to take off."

I gave the flight attendant a nod and turned off my phone. Wow, wasn't my life a shit storm at the moment? I needed to clear my head and clear it fast. What I said to my family was the truth and it had to come out sooner or later. That poor girl being pregnant with Alfie's baby and my mother dismissing it as if she was some lying piece of trash was the last straw. Actions have consequences. Now Alfie would have to live with the consequences of his disrespect for women and I would now have to live with mine. Not only with speaking the truth to my family, but also for being stupid and falling for Wyatt Coleman.

My flight landed, and I grabbed my carryon and pushed my way off the plane, running to the next gate for my flight to Los Angeles.

"Wait!" I screamed as they were about to close the plane door.

"You made it just in time," the flight attendant spoke.

I stepped onto the plane, completely out of breath as I stumbled into my first-class seat. I was exhausted, so after a couple glasses of wine, I drifted off to sleep for a while. The plane had finally landed, and I was back in Los Angeles. As soon as I turned on my phone, text messages filled my screen from Wyatt, Bella, and Craig.

Wyatt: *I'm assuming you went back to Seattle. Call me when you get home, I don't care what time it is.*

Bella: *Hey, sis. I'm so sorry for what happened. Please call me. Everything is so bad here. Celia threw her ring at Alfie and told him she never wanted to see him again. Mom is crying. Dad is pissed as hell. I never knew you felt the way you did, and it breaks my heart. Please call me so we can talk.*

Wyatt: *Laurel, please call me. I need to talk to you.*

Wyatt: *God, I fucking hate the way you left. You shouldn't be alone after everything that happened.*

Wyatt: *I'm worried about you, and I'm doing something I've never done before. I'm begging here, Laurel. Call me. Please.*

The Interview: New York & Los Angeles

Craig: *I'm standing outside the doors of baggage claim. I can't wait to see you.*

I sighed as my heart continued to ache. The only thing I cared about at the moment was seeing Craig. I arrived at baggage claim, and as I approached the glass sliding doors, Craig was standing there with his hand held up. I stopped for a moment as a smile crossed my lips. The doors opened, and I ran into his arms as he held me tight.

"Hey there," he whispered as he kissed the side of my head.

"Hey there."

He grabbed my carryon bag and hooked his arm around my neck, pulling me into him as we walked to his car.

"Are you going to tell me what happened back in Boston?" he asked as we climbed into his car.

"It wasn't only Boston. It started when I left here and went to New York. I fell in love, Craig." I glanced over at him.

"Laurel Holloway fell in love? How?" He smirked.

The whole way back to his houseboat, I told him all about Wyatt.

"You know, I haven't known him that long, but I felt this really strong connection to him and all these emotions just rose up to the surface and there was nothing I could do."

"I know the feeling." He placed his hand on my knee. "That's how I feel about Maddy. I felt it the moment my eyes first laid sight on her. If you weren't there to bring us together and me to my senses, I'd still be admiring her from afar. But you, you dove right in with Wyatt. That's how strong your connection was."

"I know. I'm such an idiot." I shook my head.

"No, you're not. We can't help who we fall in love with,

Laurel."

"I've managed all these years."

"And to be honest, I don't think it's because you wouldn't let yourself. You just never connected with the right man until him."

"I connected with you." I smiled as I lightly hit his arm.

"We connected sexually and emotionally as friends. It sounds like you connected with him on a much deeper level and quickly, may I add."

"Yeah. I know. It sucks. But I have to forget about him. He doesn't feel the same way."

"And you know that for sure?" He glanced over at me.

"If he did, he wouldn't have lied to me about his meeting and he would have called me or kept in touch. It never would have worked anyway. We're too many miles apart and we're both busy with our careers."

"You never know. Two people who are meant to be together have a way of making things work."

We reached his houseboat and he took my bag inside and placed it in the spare bedroom.

"Now tell me what happened with your family."

I took in a deep breath as I sat down on the bed and told him everything that happened. He was shocked, to say the least.

"You did what you had to do, Laurel. Don't be ashamed of it. It's been years of pent-up anger and resentment. It was bound to come out sooner or later."

"I think I destroyed my family."

He reached over and took hold of my hand.

The Interview: New York & Los Angeles

"Your family destroyed themselves. You just got caught in the crossfire. Don't forget that." He leaned over and kissed the side of my head. "Get some sleep and we'll talk about this more in the morning. You've had a long day."

"Thanks, Craig. I'm glad I came here tonight." I smiled.

"Me too. It's really good to see you again."

Chapter Thirty-Four

Craig and I spent the next day together, talking, laughing and hanging out. He took me by the restaurant on the way to the airport, so I could say hello to everyone. I had my phone turned off all day because I didn't want to deal with any incoming phone calls or text messages. I felt bad for not calling George, but he was with Veronica in Lake Tahoe and I wasn't about to ruin his trip with my problems. I'd explain everything to him tomorrow.

"Have a safe flight home," Craig spoke as he hugged me tight.

"Thanks. I have a lot of thinking to do. I just feel like I need to get away and find myself."

"Then do it." He smiled. "I think everyone needs to do that from time to time."

I reached up and kissed his cheek.

"I love you, friend."

"I love you too, friend. Text me when you land so I know you made it back."

"I will. Tell Maddy I said hi, and I'm sorry I missed her."

"Will do." He grinned.

When I got to my gate, there was still some time before I

The Interview: New York & Los Angeles

boarded, so I took a seat in a chair and turned on my phone. A new voicemail alert flashed on my screen. I opened it and brought my phone up to my ear.

"Laurel, it's Wyatt. I know you're mad at me and I don't like the way we left things. I can't force you to call me back, so I'm just going to say it here, over voicemail. I'm sorry for everything, and I didn't mean to hurt you. You're the last person I'd ever want to hurt. I just wanted you to know that. Please call me."

Tears rolled down my cheeks hearing his voice and my heartbreak intensified. I didn't want to hear his excuse as to why he lied about his meeting or why he didn't call me when I got back. I thought I needed closure, but I didn't. I only needed to get away from everything and everyone. I had some serious soul searching to do and I had made the decision that I was going to do it.

The next morning, I rolled out of bed and decided to call Bella before I headed to the office.

"Hey, I was hoping to hear from you," she answered.

"Hi. How are you?"

"I'm okay. The question is, how are you?"

"I'm hanging in there. I'm sure that's one Holloway party everyone will be talking about for a long time."

Bella let out a light laugh. "I'm sure they will be. Laurel, I don't blame you for the things you said. You had every right to say what you did. I was sick of all the secrets too. It's time our family came clean and dealt with their issues."

"Do you think Mom and Dad will get divorced now?" I asked.

"Nah. Too much of a hassle. Mom will drag it out for years. Who knows, maybe what you said to them was an eye opener and they'll work things out."

"Don't get your hopes up, little sister. I'll try to come visit you in New York from time to time, but I won't be going back to Boston anymore. I'm sure Mom and Dad have disowned me."

"No, they didn't, Laurel. They would never do that. As soon as they calm down and come to their senses, they'll be calling you."

"I'm not holding my breath. Anyway, I have to get to work. We'll talk soon."

"Promise, Laurel?"

"Yeah. I promise."

I was tired because I was up pretty much the whole night planning my trip. I wasn't sure how well this was going to go over with Eric, but he'd have to understand or else I'd quit. This was too important to me and something I needed to do.

I arrived at the office and talked to George first about everything. I told him what happened with Wyatt and my family and my plans for my upcoming trip.

"I'm so sorry I wasn't there for you." He hugged me.

"You're not responsible for always being there for me."

"I know, but I love you so much and it kills me to see you hurting."

"I'll be okay, George."

"I'm going to miss you like crazy."

"I'm going to miss you too."

"Good luck telling Eric." A smirk crossed his face.

"Come with me," I begged.

The Interview: New York & Los Angeles

"Sorry, my love, but this one you have to do alone." He kissed my forehead and walked out of my office.

"Coward!" I shouted.

I took in a deep breath and headed into Eric's office.

"Hey, Eric. Can I talk to you for a minute or two or three?"

"Sure, Laurel. How was your trip?"

"That's kind of what I need to talk to you about." I bit down on my bottom lip.

"Uh-oh. What happened?"

I told him a shortened version and then took in a deep breath.

"I need to take a personal leave of absence."

"Laurel, I'm sorry about what happened, but how long are you talking about?" he asked with concern.

"I'm going on a month-long retreat to a monastery in Thailand."

"A month? No way. I can't give you that much time off. A week maybe, but not a month."

"It's a personal leave of absence, Eric. I need this."

"Why? Can't you just go to a spa for a couple of days? Come on, Laurel."

Tears filled my eyes. "I need this," I spoke in a low voice. "And if you can't let me go, then I have no choice but to quit."

"Whoa, stop that shit!" He put his hands up. "Fine. Go. Go to Thailand, get your shit together, and get back here. A monastery, huh?"

"Yeah. I need to get away and totally disconnect from the world. And I know how hard it's going to be for you, but you can't call me. I have to give them my phone when I get there, and I can't have it back until I leave."

He looked down and started rubbing his forehead.

"When are you leaving?"

"Three days."

"Okay. Personal leave of absence granted. But you better come back." He pointed at me.

"I will." I smiled. "Thank you, Eric."

"You're welcome, kid. Now get out of here and go do some work before you leave. I want a month's worth of Everything Laurel on my desk before you board that plane."

I got up from my seat, walked over to him, and kissed his cheek.

"You got it, boss."

****

One Month Later

The moment my plane landed in Seattle, a smile crossed my face. As much as I loved Thailand, it felt so good to be home. The one thing I couldn't wait for was to sleep in my big, warm, comfy bed. I felt good, rejuvenated and at peace.

"God, I'm so happy you're back," George spoke as he hugged me tight.

"Thank you. It's good to be back." I smiled.

He drove me home and helped me with my bags.

"Anything new and exciting happen while I was gone?"

"Umm. Nope. Same old stuff."

The Interview: New York & Los Angeles

His answer sounded hesitant and I had a feeling there was something he wasn't telling me.

"Nothing at all?"

"Nope."

"You're lying. I know when you lie." I pointed at him.

"You're exhausted from your flight and you're being paranoid. Get some rest." He kissed my forehead. "I'll see you at work tomorrow."

I sighed as I went into the bathroom and started the water for a bath before I went to bed for the night. After changing into my pajamas, I decided to facetime Craig to let him know I was back.

"Laurel!" His handsome face appeared on the screen with a wide grin. "You're back?"

"Hi, Craig. I just got in a couple hours ago."

"How are you? God, it's good to hear from you."

"I'm really good. Thailand was awesome."

"Glad to hear it." He smiled. "You look great."

"Oh, please. It's okay to tell me I look like a hot mess from that flight. How's Maddy?"

"She's really good. In fact, we're really good. I feel like my life is back on track. I love her so much, Laurel."

"Aw, Craig. I'm so happy for you. Maybe I missed my calling in life. I need to quit being a journalist and go into the matchmaking business. What do you think?" I grinned.

He let out a chuckle. "I think you'd be amazing at it. I really don't want to bring it up, but I feel like I have to. How are you feeling about you know who?"

"I'm in a good place. I did a lot soul searching at the monastery. I've dealt with my feelings about relationships and my family. There was a lot of sadness and crying at first, but then everything clicked, and I've made peace with it all. For the first time in my life, I feel like I have clarity where my life is concerned."

"I'm happy to hear that, Laurel." He smiled. "You deserve nothing but happiness and I want that for you."

"I am happy, Craig." I grinned. "And I'm also exhausted, so I'm heading to bed. Tell Maddy I said hi and I'm going to try to come for a visit soon."

"I hope so. Or maybe we can come to you. We've been talking about getting away for a few days. Get some rest and we'll talk soon."

I ended the call, placed my phone on my nightstand, sank into my comfortable bed, and slept like a baby.

The Interview: New York & Los Angeles

Chapter Thirty-Five

"There's my girl." Eric smiled as he hugged me. "Welcome back, Laurel. You look great. Much better than when you left here."

"Thanks, Eric. I feel great and I'm excited to get back to work. I have so many ideas for the magazine that I need to run by you."

"Have a seat. There's something I need to discuss with you."

I didn't like the way he sounded, and a nervousness rose up inside me.

"What's up?" I asked as I sat down across from his desk.

"Some things happened here while you were away."

"Like?" I cocked my head.

"We sold the magazine division."

"What? Why?" My brows furrowed.

"An offer was made the higher ups couldn't refuse."

"Who bought it?"

"A company called Timeline Publications, Inc. They're based in New York."

"Okay, so we'll just keep doing what we were doing before

225

the magazine. Not a big deal, right?"

"Laurel, the company that bought the magazine wants me to run it and I want you and George to come with me."

"To New York? As in move there permanently?"

"Yes. They made me an offer I couldn't refuse. As much as I love working for the *Seattle Times*, I think it's time for a change. Change is good for the soul. I'm sure you learned that in the monastery. I need you with me."

"Eric." I shook my head. "I don't know. I've built a life here."

"Listen, darling. You're not tied to anyone here. You can build a great life in New York."

"And George?"

"George is on board with it but will only go if you go. Think about it, Laurel, we'll be running a magazine. Making it our own. With you and George on my team, we can do great things. You'll be making a lot more money. This company is willing to pay well."

"But it's in New York, Eric. That's the last place I want to be, let alone move there permanently."

"I know, and I thought about that. But this is an excellent opportunity for you. Didn't you learn anything at that monastery?"

"Of course, I did."

"Then put your practices to use. Embrace the change and start a new life. It's time to spread your wings."

"I'll think about it." I got up from my seat.

"You have until tomorrow, Laurel. I'm sorry, but the company wants us out there as soon as possible."

The Interview: New York & Los Angeles

"And what about my condo?"

"They said they would take care of everything for us. They'll put our houses up on the market and pay for all moving expenses."

"I'll think about it," I spoke as I walked out of his office and into George's. "You're on board with New York?" I spoke without even saying good morning.

"You talked to Eric I take it."

"Why didn't you tell me?" I snapped at him.

"Because you had just gotten back from your trip and Eric threatened me if I told you. He wanted to be the one to talk to you about it. I'll only go if you go. This is something we should do together."

"And what about Veronica?"

"She's actually excited and has already started looking for a job there. She loves New York and it's closer to her parents. Laurel, I know why you're hesitant, and I get it. I really do. But, you can't turn down a great opportunity because of one person."

"I'm over him and that whole thing."

"Okay. Then what's the problem? Is it because your sister is there?"

"No."

"You'll be closer to your family?"

"I don't have a family anymore, George. No one has even bothered to try and contact me."

"You have a family, Laurel. We're your family and we'll be there with you. You won't be doing this alone. In fact, maybe we can move into the same apartment building." He smiled as he walked over to me and grabbed my hands. "This is a good opportunity for us."

"What did your dad say about all this?"

"He told me to do what I want. He thinks it's an amazing opportunity and I should go for it. But I'll only go if you do. If you stay, I stay."

"Eric gave me until tomorrow to give him my decision. I have to do some work now. We'll talk later."

"Don't overthink it, Laurel," he shouted as I walked out of his office.

After the work day ended, I went home and gave a great deal of thought about accepting the job and moving to New York. Once I meditated and tamed the chaos in my head, the answer I sought out was clear.

****

I spent the last three weeks packing up my condo. We didn't need to worry about finding an apartment because the company owned an apartment building on East 34th Street, which had apartments available for rent. I googled the apartment building, because what if I didn't like the apartment? I wasn't about to live in something I didn't like. But it looked amazing and I was actually starting to get excited about the move, even though deep down inside, I still had some reservations. What would I do if I saw Wyatt on the street? Should I or shouldn't I tell him that I was moving there? Those were the questions I pondered every single day and meditated on them. The answers I got: Wyatt Coleman was my past and that was where I needed to keep him.

The moving truck with my boxes and furniture had already left for New York a few days ago and everything should be there when I arrived. It was the crack of dawn when George, Veronica, and I had to be at the airport for our six thirty a.m. flight. Eric had already been in New York for over a week getting things set up. By the time we arrived and made our way

The Interview: New York & Los Angeles

to our apartments, it was five p.m. It didn't help that our layover in Atlanta was delayed by an hour.

I stepped off the elevator onto the eighteenth floor and found apartment 18C. As I slid the key into the lock, I took in a deep breath and opened the door to my new home. White walls with white crown molding and light maple floor greeted me as I stepped inside. My furniture was placed neatly while all my boxes sat stacked against the wall. Even my TV was hung on the wall. Walking into the bedroom, my bed was set up with my nightstands on each side and my dresser sat against the wall next to the closet. I walked over to the large window and looked out at the city that was now going to become a part of me. New city, new job, new start.

The next morning, George and I headed to the building where the magazine was located at West 57th Street around eight a.m. Eric was there to greet us when we arrived with a huge grin across his face.

"Who's excited about this? I know I am. This is going to be great!" He hugged us both.

He showed us around, introduced us to the rest of the staff, and showed us our new offices, which were right next to each other. We spent the day going over operations and ideas for articles that would make the magazine stand out. It was five o'clock and I needed to get home to get ready for a welcome party that was being thrown tonight at The Roof for the magazine at eight o'clock.

"I'm heading home now, Eric. I'll see you later."

"Don't be late, Laurel, and by the way, good work today." He smiled.

After touching up my makeup and throwing some curls into the ends of my hair, I slipped into my pastel pink spaghetti-strap lace-fitted dress with a delicate sweetheart neckline and gave myself one more look over before sharing a cab with George and Veronica to The Roof.

"Are we finally going to be able to meet the owner tonight?" I asked George. "I'd like to meet the man responsible for making this change in our lives."

"I'm not sure. I would think he'd be here."

"I'm heading over to the bar," I spoke.

"I'll meet you there in a minute. I need to ask Eric something," George said as we parted ways.

I walked over to the bar and waited for the bartender, who was helping someone else, come over and take my drink order.

"What can I get you, miss?" he asked.

"She'll have a neat martini straight up with two olives," a voice behind me spoke and suddenly I became paralyzed. "You look absolutely stunning, Laurel."

I couldn't turn around. My heart was racing at the speed of light and a sick feeling formed in the pit of my belly.

"What are you doing here, Wyatt?" I asked without looking at him.

I grabbed the glass out of the bartender's hand before he had a chance to set it down and took a large drink.

"Aren't you even going to look at me?" he asked.

I slowly turned around and stared at the six-foot three sexy man dressed in a tailored black designer suit. A smile swept across his face as our eyes locked on each other's.

"Can we have that talk now?" he asked.

"Hey, Laurel." George walked over to us.

"Hello there, I'm Wyatt Coleman." He extended his hand.

"Oh. Um, George Locke." He lightly shook it. "You okay, Laurel?"

The Interview: New York & Los Angeles

"I'm fine." I finished off my drink.

"I'll leave you two to talk, then." He walked away and a part of me wished he wouldn't have.

"What talk are you referring to, Wyatt?" I asked as I signaled for the bartender to bring me another drink.

"The one I begged you to have with me back in Boston."

"For God sakes, Wyatt, let it go already. If I wanted to listen to your lame excuse as to why you lied to me about your meeting and why you didn't call me after I left, I would have done it by now. That's all in the past and that's where it's staying. Like I said to you before, if my absence didn't affect you, then my presence had no meaning." I walked away, and he lightly grabbed my arm, pulling me close to him.

"Your absence did affect me and that's what I'm trying to tell you. Now, can we have that talk?" He cocked his head.

"Listen, this is a work party. Wait a minute." I shook my head. "Why aren't you asking me what I'm doing in New York? You don't even seem shocked that I'm here. And what the hell are you doing at my work party?" I narrowed my eye at him.

"I can explain that too."

Suddenly, a lightbulb went off in my head.

"No!" I shook my finger at him. "Oh hell no. I'm going to ask you a question and I want you to tell me the truth. If you don't tell me the truth, I will never speak to you again. Do you understand me?"

"I don't appreciate the way you're talking to me, but fine, I will tell you nothing but the truth."

"Are you the one who bought the magazine and brought me here to New York?"

He stood there for a moment, staring into my eyes while he

took in a deep breath.

"Yes."

One simple word. That was all he said. One word that changed my entire life.

"You bastard." I slowly shook my head as I raised my hand to slap him, but he grabbed it before I had the chance.

"I knew you were going to try and do that."

I yanked myself from his grip.

"Don't touch me." I pointed at him. "You're crazy if you think I'm going to talk to you. Especially now."

"Okay, fine. I didn't want to do this and make a scene in front of all these people, but you've given me no choice," he spoke as he picked me up and threw me over his shoulder.

"What the fuck do you think you're doing? Put me down." I started pounding on his back.

"Nope. I'm going to speak and you're going to listen. You're not winning this one."

He carried me down the stairs and out of the bar. I had never been so humiliated in my life as everyone stopped and stared. Once we were outside, Ryan opened the door to the limo and Wyatt put me inside, climbing in next to me and then shutting and locking the door.

"Drive, Ryan," Wyatt spoke.

"You're a goddamn psychopath!" I yelled at him.

"No. You're just being unreasonable, and as soon as you calm down, we can talk. I gave you enough chances to call me and you refused."

"So, because I didn't call you back, you resort to

The Interview: New York & Los Angeles

kidnapping?"

"This isn't kidnapping, Laurel. Don't be ridiculous. You're free to go at any time after we talk."

"That's what kidnappers say after they get the information they want." I cocked my head at him.

"Like I said, you're not winning this one, sweetheart." He smirked.

I closed my eyes, took in four long, deep breaths, and sat completely still.

"What are you doing?" Wyatt asked.

"Shh. I'm meditating. Do not say another word."

"Why are you doing that right now?"

"It's to prevent me from killing you. Now shush!"

A light chuckle escaped him. After a few moments, I took in one last deep breath, let it out, opened my eyes, and glanced over at him.

"I'm ready to listen to you. Where would you like to have this conversation?" I calmly asked.

"Anywhere you want," he spoke.

"Central Park."

"I was hoping somewhere a little more private, but if you want to talk in Central Park, then fine. Any specific area?"

"Nope. Anywhere is fine," I replied.

"I think I know the perfect spot. Ryan, drop us off at 72nd and Central Park West."

"Very well, Mr. Coleman."

"Thank you, Laurel." He reached over and placed his hand on mine.

An electrifying shock tore through me, just like it always did when he touched me. I pulled my hand out from under his.

"Don't, Wyatt."

We sat there in silence until we reached 72nd and Central Park West. We walked for a while until we reached Cherry Hill and we both took a seat on the bench that overlooked the lake.

"Had I known I was going to be doing all this walking, I would have worn better shoes," I spoke as I took off my heels.

"Sorry about that, but you wanted to talk in Central Park."

"Now that you've successfully kidnapped me and tortured me in heels, you better start talking."

The Interview: New York & Los Angeles

Chapter Thirty-Six

"I've been preparing for this talk for quite a while," he spoke. "To be honest, Laurel, you scare me."

I let out a light laugh.

"You're not the first, Wyatt."

"I don't mean physically. I mean emotionally. Damn it, this is a lot harder than I thought it would be." He got up from the bench, tucked his hands in his pockets, and paced around. "From the moment I saw you in the airport, when you handed me my coffee, I felt this incredible pull towards you. I dismissed it as you being another beautiful woman whom I didn't have time for because I had a plane to catch and walked away. Then, you were there again, on the plane, sitting in the seat across from me. I wanted you sexually, and I knew you wanted me too."

"That was very presumptuous of you." I arched my brow at him.

"Yeah, well, if I wasn't one hundred percent sure, I wouldn't have taken you to the bathroom. I don't do anything unless I'm sure, so don't try to deny it."

"I'm not denying anything," I spoke.

"After we had sex, there was a part of me that wanted to ask you out while you were staying in New York, which never happens, but you were there to see your sister in Swan Lake and I didn't want to disrupt any plans that you already had. It was true that my sister wanted to go, and after you told me you were going to be there, I bought the tickets with the hopes that I'd get a chance to see you."

"Why?" I asked.

"Just let me finish. To say the least, I was shocked when you told me off and didn't let me get a word in edgewise, and as much as I wanted to run after you and tell you that Sammi was my sister, I let it go because I thought I'd never see you again. Hell, I didn't even know your name. I couldn't stop thinking about you that whole night or the next day. Then Monday morning, when I opened my office door and saw you standing there, I couldn't believe my eyes. I thought maybe you found out who I was and came to my office to finish telling me off. When you told me who you really were and why you were there, I used it to my advantage to keep you in New York as long as I could."

"So, you had already made up your mind at that point that you were granting me the interview?" I asked.

"Yes. Because I knew that I would be able to spend some more time with you. Those few days with you were some of the best times of my life, Laurel."

"Then why didn't you want to take me to the airport? And why did you wait to say goodbye at the last minute as you were leaving for the office? You could have woken me up and we could have spent that morning together before I left."

"Because I didn't want to say goodbye, and I knew once you boarded that plane, it was over. So, I just had to let you go as quickly as possible. I was protecting myself because things were happening inside me that weren't very clear to me. After you left, I couldn't stop thinking about you. My days and nights became very lonely, and I knew if we stayed in contact, it would only make things worse."

The Interview: New York & Los Angeles

"Well, I'm glad one of us was protecting themselves," I spoke with an attitude.

He stopped pacing and took a seat beside me on the bench.

"I needed to be sure about you," he spoke. "I needed to be one hundred percent sure of my feelings, and the longer I went without seeing you and talking to you, the surer I became. But still, we were faced with the distance. Me in New York and you in Seattle, so I knew I needed to put a plan into action. Timeline Publications was going under and fast, so I bought them with the plan of bringing *Daily Fusion* to New York. That morning we ran into each other, I was signing the final paperwork with the lawyer."

"At a restaurant?"

"Yes. We met halfway because she had another meeting right around the corner and it didn't make sense for her to come all the way to my office."

"How the hell did my brother's engagement party come into play?" I asked.

"To be honest, I have no clue. Your father just called me up and invited me. I wasn't going to go because I thought you wouldn't attend. But when your sister said the two of you were driving there, I knew it would be my chance to talk to you. I was going to tell you how I felt and about my plans for the magazine that night, but then all that shit went down with your family. When you refused to call me back, I called Eric and he told me you were taking a month-long personal leave of absence and going to Thailand. I flew out to Seattle and made the VPs of the magazine division an offer they couldn't refuse. I also convinced them that combining the paper and magazine in one company wasn't a good idea. I needed to act quickly while you were gone."

"Oh." I looked down. "How did you know that I would accept the job and move here? That was huge risk you took, Wyatt."

"I know, and trust me, that thought plagued me every day. But I knew how close you were to Eric and George. He did nothing but sing your praises and tell me how important you were to him when we met. And even though he was your boss, I sensed you considered him family too. So, if I could get them to come, I knew you'd follow. Plus, I checked into Eric and I think he's an incredible asset to the magazine, as well as you and George."

"You're telling me that Eric and George knew about all of this prior and I didn't?"

"Only Eric did, not George. I told him that everything stayed between us. I was afraid if you caught wind that I was the one behind it all, you wouldn't come."

"So, you two deceived me? Why not? Everyone else in my life seems to."

"God, Laurel. No. I mean, I guess I can see where you're coming from. I needed to make things right with you and I was planning on doing that at your parents' house, but you wouldn't let me. I wanted to comfort you and tell you that everything was going to be okay."

I didn't know what it was I felt at that moment. It was a mixture of all kinds of emotions that were all banging into one another like a pile up on the expressway. I got up from the bench.

"And you thought it would be okay to just disrupt my life and uproot me from Seattle because YOU needed to make things right?" I shouted as I pointed at him.

"What other fucking choice did I have?" he shouted back as he got up from the bench and threw his arms out. "You refused to talk to me!"

"Because you broke my heart!" I yelled as tears filled my eyes. "And I knew if I let you explain, I'd fall for you all over again and I couldn't let that happen. That night I had the panic attack, it was because of you. Because all these feelings for you came out of nowhere and it scared the fuck out of me. Then when I left, you acted like you didn't care, and that was something I had to deal with alone."

"But I did care, and I need you to understand why I did what I did." He took a few steps closer to me. "Laurel, we're both fucked up. Neither one of us would open our hearts to anyone. Then we were thrown together by some sort of fate and we both kind of got blindsided. You know I'm right because you just admitted your feelings for me sent you into a panic attack. You didn't come to New York to fall in love and I sure as hell wasn't looking for anything. But something between us happened and it's something neither of us could deny, no matter how hard we tried."

I sighed as I covered my face with my hands and sat back down on the bench.

"I never said I fell in love," I softly spoke, even though I had.

"Maybe it's too early for that." He sat next to me. "But I sure as hell know, without a doubt in my mind, I need you in my life and not long distance either. I need to see you every day. I need to see your smile and hear your laughter. I need to know you'll be there when I'm having a bad day and all I want to do is wrap my arms around you and hold you tight. This is all new to me, Laurel, and I'm expressing it as best I can. I've never had such strong feelings, or any type of feelings for any woman as I do you. Do you remember at the ballet when you said to me that one day I'll actually love someone, and they'll hurt me and it'll break my heart, and when that day comes, you hope I'll think of you?"

"Yes, I remember." I pulled my hands away from my face and stared at him.

"Well, it happened, and I did think of you because you're the one that broke it. It broke my heart when you left New York."

I was crying on the outside, but on the inside, I was relieved and happy. He did love me, but what kind of person would I be if I just jumped into his arms and forgave everything he did right away. For God sakes, he bought a company so he could move me to New York. Who does that? It was the sweetest thing anyone had ever done for me. Was it wrong to go behind my back and not discuss it with me first? Yes. Could I forgive him for that? Eventually. But he had to learn that just because he was a billionaire, he couldn't get everything he wanted with the snap of his fingers.

I wiped the tears that fell down my face.

"I need time to process all this and to think."

"I understand."

"Can I ask you a question? I need you to be very honest with me, even if you think it might hurt me."

"Of course."

"How many women have you slept with since I left?"

A small smile crossed his lips as he brought his hand up to my cheek.

"None. The last time I had sex was with you the night before you left."

"How is that possible?" I narrowed my eye at him.

"Well, let's just say my hand hurts like a bitch. How about you? How many men have you slept with since you left?"

"None. I was too heartbroken."

"I'm sorry." He stroked my cheek and I wanted to rip his clothes off right there and have sex on the bench. "Will you forgive me, Laurel?"

"Like I said, Wyatt, I need time."

The Interview: New York & Los Angeles

"How much time are you thinking?"

In my head, I was thinking as much time as it took to drive him insane.

"I don't know yet. If it's okay, I'd like to go home."

"Of course."

Chapter Thirty-Seven

George thought I was crazy. Veronica told me it was all about girl power. Eric pretty much hid from me for a couple of days because he was scared, and Craig laughed and said he wasn't surprised by me keeping Wyatt waiting.

A week had passed since our talk, and we hadn't seen each other at all. My choice. But to be honest, I didn't know how much longer I could hold out. Teaching him a lesson was also hurting me. We'd text quite a bit during the day and talk on the phone for at least two hours every night. I finally called Bella and told her that I moved to New York. She was happy and promised not to tell our parents. The same parents whom I hadn't heard a word from since that night.

It was three o'clock on a Friday and I was standing outside my office talking to George and Eric going over some edit copies when I looked up and saw Wyatt coming down the hallway. My heart started racing, for I had no clue why he was here. He walked up to me, and Eric and George stepped out of the way.

"Wyatt—"

He placed his hand on each side of my face and smashed his mouth against mine.

"You've punished me enough," he said after he broke our kiss.

The Interview: New York & Los Angeles

He leaned down, placed his hands under my legs, and swooped me up in his arms.

"What are you doing?" I smiled.

"Taking you out of here for the weekend. She won't be in on Monday, Eric," he spoke as he carried me down the hallway.

"Whatever you say, boss. Have fun, Laurel!"

My arms stayed securely around his neck as our lips kept touching.

"And where are we going?"

"To the ranch, where nobody will disturb us for a few days. It'll just be me and you, baby." He smiled.

****

He hovered over me, thrusting in and out like a wild beast while sweat encased our bodies. We were both out of breath, but we didn't care. We kept going at it like it was our last day on Earth.

"Holy shit!" he exclaimed as he poured himself inside me for the third time and then his body collapsed on mine.

"Holy shit is right. I still feel like I'm orgasming."

He lifted his head up and smiled as he pressed his lips against mine.

"Good. I want you to feel that way forever."

"I want to feel this way forever." I brought my hand up and ran it through his hair.

He rolled off me and onto his back as I snuggled against him. It felt so good to be back in his strong arms again.

"There's something I feel like I should tell you," I spoke.

"What is it?"

"The night I left Boston, I flew to Los Angeles to see Craig."

"Why?"

"Because he's a good friend of mine and I needed to talk to him."

"Okay. Did the two of you sleep together? Because you told me that you hadn't slept with anyone since you left New York."

Shit. I knew he was going to ask me that.

"I didn't sleep with him that night. But I did sleep with him before." I sat up and looked at him.

"Why are you telling me this?" he asked.

"Because I don't want there to be any secrets between us."

"I see. Well, what you did before we met is none of my business. It sounds like the two of you are close."

"We are." I smiled. "As friends. Actually, he had some relationship issues that I helped him with."

I explained the whole story to him and he lay there with a smile on his face.

"Why am I not surprised at all by what you told me? But I will admit, I'm a little shocked that you followed him to the cemetery and hid behind other people's gravestones. I always figured you for a stalker." He smirked.

I smacked him with the pillow.

"He wouldn't tell me what was going on, so I had to find out for myself."

"Well, I'm happy you helped him out. I can't even imagine what he was going through. This is why I love you. You just do and say what's on your mind without a care in the world. You're strong, sassy, beautiful, caring, and you don't take shit from anyone, including me." His brow raised.

"Did you just say you loved me?" I smiled as I cocked my head.

"Yes, I did." He grinned. "But I didn't say it to you properly, so let me say it again. I love you, Laurel Holloway. I didn't just fall in love with your beauty, I fell in love with your soul." He brought his hand up to my cheek and softly stroked it.

Tears filled my eyes and I swallowed hard.

"I love you too, Wyatt Coleman."

I leaned over and brushed my lips against his as his arm wrapped around my waist.

****

Eight Months Later

Wyatt and I were as happy as two people could be. I honestly didn't think that people could be that happy. I ended up publishing the articles on Craig and Wyatt for the magazine with a six-month update on both their statuses. The two of them became good friends after we flew out to California to spend some time with him and Maddy. Wyatt was trying to convince him to open up a restaurant in New York, which he was seriously considering. The two of them talked more than Craig and I did.

About three months after I moved to New York, Wyatt suggested that I move in with him. I spent pretty much ninety-nine percent of my time at his place as it was, and the one percent I wasn't there, or he wasn't at my place didn't feel right.

It was a Saturday morning and I awoke to the sound of the shower on. Climbing out of bed, I walked into the bathroom, opened the glass door and stepped inside, wrapping my arms around Wyatt's neck.

"Good morning." He smiled as he kissed my lips.

"Good morning. Why didn't you wake me?"

"Because you looked so beautiful and peaceful. You should sleep in. It's Saturday."

"I can't sleep when you're not in bed with me." I pouted as my finger lightly ran down his chest.

"I know the feeling."

He grabbed the bottle of shampoo, poured some into his hand, and worked it through my hair.

"I wish you didn't have to go in to the office today," I spoke.

"I know, but I'll be home early. This deal is almost done. What are you going to do today?"

"I need to go find a dress for Craig and Maddy's wedding."

"Are you going alone?"

"Yes. I don't want to be gone all day. In and out." I smiled. "One store only."

"Good luck with that. Now turn around." He grinned, and I felt the forceful thrust of his cock inside me.

Wyatt left for the office and I headed out the door and over to Fifth Avenue. Four stores so far and nothing.

"Hello there, sexy." I smiled as Wyatt's face appeared on the screen.

"Any luck finding a dress yet?"

"No." I pouted. "I'm heading over to Chanel now to see if they have something."

"I'm sure you'll find something there. I just wanted to say hi. I love you and I miss you. I need to get back to my meeting."

The Interview: New York & Los Angeles

"I love and miss you too. See you later."

I approached the Chanel store, and when I stepped inside, a tall gentleman with blonde slicked-back hair approached me.

"Good day, Madame," he spoke with a French accent. "How can I assist you today?"

"Good day. I'm looking for a dress for a wedding I'm attending next month."

"Ah, we have a wonderful selection. Follow me. My name is Francois and you are?"

"Laurel Holloway." I smiled.

He took me to over to the selection of dresses and pulled out what he thought would look best on me. As I was looking the dresses over, I froze when I heard a familiar voice in the distance.

Oh hell no.

I slowly turned around and saw my mother walking my way with another sales associate.

"Francois." I grabbed his arm. "You need to hide me, now!"

"Excuse me, Madame?"

"No time to explain." I ducked behind a display, pulling him down with me.

"What is going on?"

"That woman over there is my mother and I can't let her see me."

"Oh. Why?" He gave me a confused look.

"Long story, but we haven't spoken in almost a year. I knew when I moved here I'd run into her eventually."

"The fitting rooms are right behind us. Come with me and I'll quickly get you into one."

As I tried to stay low to the ground, I followed Francois and he opened the fitting room door.

"Stay in here until the coast is clear. I'll keep watch for you and I'll bring you dresses to try on."

"Thank you."

I sat down in the round comfy chair and pulled out my phone, sending a text message to Wyatt.

"My mother is here in Chanel!"

"What? Did she see you?"

"No. Me and Francois ducked behind a display and now I'm in the fitting room."

"Who's Francois?"

"The French salesman who was helping me find a dress. He's on guard and is going to let me know when she leaves."

"Good. Keep me posted. I should be done here soon. I can meet you."

"Okay. I'd love that. Just text me. Who knows, the way she shops, I may be in here for hours."

Francois brought me a couple of dresses to try on. They weren't bad, but they weren't really my style.

"Madame, the coast is clear. She's gone."

I opened the door and handed him the dresses.

"Sadly, these didn't work for me. But I love these pants over here." I pulled my size from the rack. "They'd be perfect for the office."

The Interview: New York & Los Angeles

"Excellent taste, Madame." He smiled.

The truth was I didn't need another pair of pants, but I felt obligated to buy something from him since he helped me. As he was ringing me up, my phone dinged with a text message from Wyatt.

"Did she leave?"

"Yes. I'm checking out now."

"I'm on my way. I'll meet you outside the store in about seven minutes."

"Okay. Love you."

"Love you too, baby."

After I completed my transaction, Francois walked me down the stairs and towards the doors, opening it for me.

"It was a pleasure hanging out with you, Laurel," he spoke.

"You too, Francois." I smiled.

"Laurel?" I heard my mother's voice from behind.

Shit. Shit. Shit.

My heart started racing as I pretended I didn't hear her and casually walked out the door, stopping dead in my tracks when I saw Wyatt standing a few feet away talking to a man that looked like my father. Wyatt stared at me for a moment with a look that was telling me to run. I turned the opposite way until my mother flew out of the store and loudly called out my name.

"Laurel Marie Holloway."

I froze in place and slowly turned around, looking beyond my mother at Wyatt and my father who were staring at me.

"Hey," I casually spoke as I walked over to her, taking in several deep breaths.

Wyatt and my father walked over to where we were standing.

"Laurel," my father spoke.

"Hey, Dad," I awkwardly replied.

"What on earth are you doing here in New York?" my mother asked with a slight attitude.

"The question is, what on earth are you two doing here?"

I wasn't answering her question and I wasn't backing down, until Wyatt cleared his throat and felt the need to step in.

"They're going to find out sooner or later," he spoke.

"Find out what?" My mother looked at him.

"Laurel lives with me here in New York."

"Since when?" my father asked.

"Oh, about eight months or so," I replied.

"Actually, we've only been living together for the past five months," Wyatt felt the need to clarify.

"Can you just be quiet?" I looked over at him.

"So, you're working in New York?" my mother asked.

"Yes."

"And why didn't you bother to tell us?" my father spoke with irritation.

"Why would I? You told me to leave your house and I haven't heard a word from you since." I started to speak in anger. "Now if you'll excuse us, Wyatt and I have shopping to do. I don't have time to stand here and explain myself or my life to two people who couldn't give a damn. Wyatt, let's go."

The Interview: New York & Los Angeles

"Laurel, wait," my father spoke. "I think it's time we talked."

"Good idea, Jefferson. We can talk back at the penthouse," Wyatt spoke.

I was going to kill him.

"Text me your address and we'll head over in about thirty minutes. I have something I need to get first," my father said.

"Laurel, Ryan is this way," Wyatt spoke as he tightly grabbed my hand, for he knew he was in trouble.

"How could you?" I spewed as we climbed into the limo.

"They want to talk, and this is going to end now. Whether it be good or bad."

"And who the hell are you to make that decision?" My eyes glared at him.

"The man who loves you more than anything in this world and hates to see you upset. That's who. So, go ahead and be mad. Hell, hate me. I don't care, Laurel. This is something the three of you need to put to rest."

As much as I hated to admit it, he was right.

"I could never be mad at you. Hate you, yes." I smirked.

He leaned over and kissed my cheek.

"Just don't hate me for too long."

Chapter Thirty-Eight

The moment I stepped inside the penthouse, I walked over to the bar and poured myself a shot of whiskey.

"You don't drink whiskey," Wyatt spoke.

"I need something strong before they get here."

"Why don't you just go meditate?" He took the shot glass from my hand and threw it down his throat.

"Good idea."

"Feel better?" Wyatt asked as I emerged from upstairs.

"I do." I walked over and gave him a kiss.

The house phone rang, which only meant one thing: my parents were here.

"Send them right up," Wyatt spoke before ending the call.

He walked over to me and placed his hands firmly on my hips and leaned his forehead against mine.

"You got this."

"I got this." I lightly smiled.

The elevator doors opened, and Wyatt went over to greet them as I stood in a calm state in the living room.

The Interview: New York & Los Angeles

"What a beautiful home," my mother spoke to Wyatt as she looked around.

"Thank you, Adalynn. Come, have a seat."

"Laurel." My mother nodded.

"Mom." I nodded back, trying to stay in my Zen state.

"Laurel, why don't you come sit down." Wyatt patted the spot next to him on the couch.

"I'll stand. Thank you." I folded my arms.

The tension in the room was thick. So thick that I didn't think anything was sharp enough to cut through it.

"You wanted to talk, Dad, so talk. I already said what I needed to that night."

"Your mother and I have put everything that we've done to each other in the past, and we're seeking therapy and working things out."

"Good for you!" I spoke in a sarcastic tone. "So, neither one of you are sleeping around anymore?" I pointed to both of them.

"No, we're not," my father spoke. "We were hoping you could put the past behind you and move on as well. You're our daughter, Laurel, and we love you. Regardless of what you said to us."

"See, Dad, the difference is you only got a few minutes of what I thought. I got a lifetime of it from her. That is something you don't ever forget."

"Adalynn," my father spoke as he glanced over at her.

My mother cleared her throat like she always did when she was uncomfortable.

"You're right, Laurel. I treated you differently than Alfie and

Bella and I apologize."

"Why?"

"Because from the time you were very little, you were so defiant, independent, and stubborn. I'd tell you to do something and you'd do the total opposite. I felt as if I had no control over you whatsoever and I used the excuse because you weren't my flesh and blood, so I gave up. But I never once stopped loving you. You're my daughter, and I'm sorry I made you feel anything less. We weren't perfect parents and I know your deep-rooted issues stemmed from us."

Wow, I couldn't believe she admitted that.

"You're right, they did."

"If you want the honest to God's truth why I always pushed you and nagged you about having a boyfriend, it's because—" She looked down.

"Because why?"

"I thought maybe you were a lesbian and I didn't think I could handle that. How would I tell our friends?"

"Oh my God, Mom!" I placed my hands on my head.

"She's definitely not a lesbian." Wyatt smiled.

"Why would you think that?" I asked.

"Because you never showed any interest in boys, not even in your peak teenage years. Then you met David in college and I was relieved. But it all started back up again after you told me the two of you broke up because you grew apart, and you never brought anyone home after that or even mentioned a guy. I thought maybe David was just an experiment. When I would ask you, you evaded the subject with some sarcastic remark. I figured you were too afraid to tell us that you like girls."

"I could never get involved with someone because of the two

The Interview: New York & Los Angeles

of you. Your relationship alone was enough to scar me for life. All your cheating and lies to each other. Then, I finally let David into my life and he turned around and broke my heart, just like the both of you did. You know what the problem with you is?" I pointed to my mother. "You give too many fucks what other people think. You've spent the last thirty years of marriage, hell, maybe your whole entire life trying to create the perfect image of yourself. But you know what, Mom? While you were doing that, you lost you. In fact, the two of you lost each other."

She sat there with her lips pressed firmly together, for she knew I was right.

"She's right, Adalynn." My father reached over and took hold of her hand.

My mother looked up at me as I stood in front of her.

"I'm sorry, Laurel, and you're right, I did lose me somewhere many years ago. I wanted to be the perfect woman with the perfect family, and in doing so, I lost my oldest daughter." Her eyes swelled with tears.

"You didn't lose me, Mom. If you did, you wouldn't be in my home right now. And nobody's perfect. Not even Wyatt."

"Hey," he chimed in.

"I know it's not too late and I have many years to undo the wrong I've done and make it right. That's if you'll let me," she spoke. "I have three children and I want us all together again. I want my family back."

"It's going to take time for that," I spoke. "It's not something we can fix overnight."

"I know that, but I hope you'll let me try."

A small smile crossed my lips as I knelt down in front of her and lightly placed my hand on hers.

"Only if you let me try."

"Of course I will." She smiled as the tears continued to fall down her face.

The four us went out for a nice dinner, compliments of Wyatt.

"He's a good catch," my mother leaned over and whispered in my ear.

"I know." I grinned. "He makes me incredibly happy."

"I can tell." She smiled as she cupped my chin with her hand.

****

One Month Later

"Craig looks nervous up there," I spoke as we sat in white satin-covered chairs on the beach waiting for the wedding ceremony to start.

"He does, doesn't he?" Wyatt smiled.

Craig glanced over at me and I gave him a thumbs-up. A smile graced his face and I took pride in the fact that I brought these two people together.

The music began to play, and everyone stood up and watched as Maddy walked down the aisle to her future husband.

"She looks so beautiful." I placed my hand over my heart. "You know, this is all happening because of me," I whispered to Wyatt.

"I know. You're quite the little matchmaker. Cemetery stalking, inviting yourself to other people's tables, and setting up false meetings. Good job, sweetheart."

I turned and looked at him with knitted brows as he chuckled.

We took our seats and listened as the minister began to

The Interview: New York & Los Angeles

speak. It was time for their wedding vows, and suddenly, I got all choked up and fought back the tears, so I didn't ruin my makeup. Wyatt glanced over at me and lightly squeezed my hand as he leaned over and whispered in my ear.

"You want to do something like this?" he asked.

"Get married?"

"Yeah."

"I don't know." I shrugged. "Do you?"

"I don't know. Could be kind of fun."

"True." I raised my brows. "Planning a wedding is a huge hassle and very stressful. My mother would try to take over."

"That's true. Do we really need that hassle and stress in our lives?" he asked.

"I don't think we do."

"Nah. Me either. Forget I mentioned it."

"Nice thought, though." I glanced over at him with a smile.

The reception was held in a large white tent on the beach, which was elegantly decorated and with only the best food catered from Craig's restaurant.

"Excuse me, can I have everyone's attention, please?" Craig spoke as he tapped his glass with a spoon.

Everyone in the tent went silent. He thanked us for coming and then gave a beautiful speech about his new bride.

"I would also like to take this opportunity to thank one of my best friends, Laurel Holloway. If it wasn't for her, we wouldn't be here today celebrating our wedding. If she hadn't conned her way into my restaurant, we never would have met. She was relentless and wouldn't give up. She was sent to interview me, and in the process of doing that, she set me straight and made me realize that life still goes on even in the depths of tragedy. She's my hero. I'm not only honored to have her in my life, but I'm also honored to call her my best friend."

Wyatt leaned over and kissed my cheek as the tears steadily fell.

"With that being said." Craig walked over to where I was sitting. "May I have this dance?" He smiled as he extended his hand to me.

"Look at me," I sniffled. "You've ruined my makeup."

"You look beautiful, Laurel." He smiled as we danced. "Look at us. Just a year ago, we were two broken people who wouldn't even think about loving someone. I think we've come a long way."

"We have, haven't we?"

"It's good to see you with Wyatt and to see you so happy. Can I let you in on a little secret? You can't tell anyone except Wyatt."

"I promise I won't. Hell, I may not even tell him." I grinned.

"Maddy is pregnant. We found out a couple days ago."

"Oh, Craig." I hugged him tight. "That's wonderful."

"Yeah. It was quite a shock, but a good one. We're going to wait a while before we announce it. Just in case, you know."

"I know. But I'm happy you told me."

"You were the first person I couldn't wait to tell."

The music ended, and I pulled my compact out of my purse and fixed my makeup. Looking around, I couldn't find Wyatt anywhere, so I walked out of the tent and found him standing by the water.

The Interview: New York & Los Angeles

"Hey, what are you doing?" I wrapped my arm around his waist.

"Just staring at the ocean." He smiled. "The sun is going to set in a few minutes."

"Ah, I love sunsets on the beach." I laid my head on his shoulder.

"You know, I got to thinking about something," he spoke.

"About what?"

"About how you're the most beautiful and precious flower in my garden."

"I better be the only beautiful and precious flower in your garden."

"Oh, you are." He smiled. "In fact, you're the rarest flower I've ever encountered. You're so rare that I can never let you go."

As heart melting and panty melting as his words were, I couldn't help but let out a light laugh.

"Good, because you're stuck with this rare flower whether you like it or not." I shoulder bumped him.

"Can you do me a favor?" he asked.

"What?"

"Close your eyes for a minute."

"Why?"

"I want you to listen to the sound of the waves crashing against the shore. There's something strange about it and I want to know if you can hear what I did."

"You're weird, but okay." I grinned.

I closed my eyes and listened carefully like he asked.

"Keep them closed and just listen. Do you hear it?"

"I don't think so. They sound pretty normal to me."

"You can open your eyes."

I slowly opened my eyes to see Wyatt kneeling down on one knee in the sand holding a small blue velvet ring box in his hand.

"See, Laurel, the thing is, I love you more than life. I thought I was happy until you came along, but it turned out I wasn't. I never knew what loneliness was until you went back to Seattle and that is something I never want to experience again. You make me laugh all the time. You always have me on my toes because I never know what the hell you're going to do next. Sometimes, you embarrass me, and I simply smile and say that's my girl. You make my life exciting because being with you is an adventure, and it's one I want to stay on for the rest of my life. I want the hassle and stress of planning a wedding because there's no other person in this world I want to spend eternity with. So, what do you say?" He flipped open the lid. "Will you marry me?"

"Ab-so-fucking-lutely!" I shouted with a smile as the tears fell from my eyes.

He removed the gorgeous platinum square diamond ring from the box and slipped it on my finger. I fell to my knees and wrapped my arms around his neck.

"I love you, Wyatt," I spoke as I brushed my lips against his.

"I love you too, baby. So very much."

"You knew I'd say yes?" I grinned.

"I was one hundred percent sure of it." He leaned his forehead against mine with a smile.

About the Author

Sandi Lynn is a *New York Times*, *USA Today* and *Wall Street Journal* bestselling author who spends all her days writing. She published her first novel, *Forever Black*, in February 2013 and hasn't stopped writing since. Her addictions are shopping, going to the gym, romance novels, coffee, chocolate, margaritas, and giving readers an escape to another world.

Be a part of my tribe!

Facebook: www.facebook.com/Sandi.Lynn.Author

Twitter: www.twitter.com/SandilynnWriter

Website: www.authorsandilynn.com

Pinterest: www.pinterest.com/sandilynnWriter

Instagram: www.instagram.com/sandilynnauthor

Goodreads: http://bit.ly/2w6tN25

My Shop: www.sandilynnromance.com

If you're interested in purchasing a signed paperback from me, click on the "My Shop" link above!

Printed in Poland
by Amazon Fulfillment
Poland Sp. z o.o., Wrocław